CLAR

MW01706063

FICTION

NON-FICTION

Neil Clarke: Publisher/Editor-in-Chief
Sean Wallace: Editor
Kate Baker: Non-Fiction Editor/Podcast Director

Clarkesworld Magazine (ISSN: 1937-7843) • Issue 144 • September 2018

A Study in Oils

KELLY ROBSON

Halfway up the winding cliffside guideway, Zhang Lei turned his bike around. He was exhausted from three days of travel and nauseated, too, but that wasn't the problem. He could always power through physical discomfort. But the trees, the rocks, the open sky above, and the mountains closing in—it was all too strange. He kept expecting something to drop on his head.

He pinged Marta, the social worker in Beijing Hive who'd orchestrated his escape from Luna seventy-two hours earlier.

Forget Paizuo, he whispered as his bike coasted the guideway's downslope. *This is too weird.*

Turn that bike back around or I'll hit your disable button, Marta whispered back.

You wouldn't.

He turned the bike's acceleration to maximum.

I would. You can spend the next two weeks lying at the bottom of a gully while the tribunal decides what to do with you. Turn around.

No, I'm going back to the Danzhai roadhouse.

When she scowled, her whole face crumpled into a mass of wrinkles. She didn't even look like a person anymore.

I'd do anything to keep you alive, kid, and I don't even like you. She jabbed at him with an age-spotted finger, as if she could reach across the continent and poke him in the chest. *Turn back around or I'll do it.*

He believed her. Nobody had hit his disable button since he'd left Luna, but Marta was an old ex-Lunite and that meant she was both tough and mean. Zhang Lei slowed his bike, rotated back to the guideway's uphill track, and gave the acceleration dial a vicious twist.

You don't like me? he asked.

Maybe a little. Marta flipped through the graphs of his biom. She had full access to that too, and could check everything from his hormone levels to his sleep cycle. *You're getting dehydrated. Drink some water. And slow your bike. You're going to make yourself puke.*

I feel fine, he lied.

Marta rolled her eyes. *Relax. You'll love Paizuo. Nobody wants to kill you there.*

She slapped the connection down, and the image of her elderly face was replaced by steep, verdant mountainside. Danzhai County was thick with an impossible greenness, in layers of bushes, trees, grasses, and herbs he had no name for.

Everything was unfamiliar here. He knew he was deep in southwestern China, but that's about all. He knew he was surrounded by mountains, with Danzhai's transit hub behind him. It was a two-pad skip station, the smallest he'd ever seen, next to a narrow lake surrounded by hills, everything green but the sky—which actually was blue, like everyone always said about Earth—and the buildings. Those were large, brown, and open to the air as if atmospheric weather was nothing.

An atmosphere people could breathe. That was Earth's one unique claim. Unlike Luna, or Venus, or Mars, or any of the built environments in the solar system, here in Danzhai and a few other places on Earth, humans lived every day exposed to weather. It was traditional, or something.

Weather was overrated, Zhang Lei decided. The afternoon was so humid, he'd sweated through his shirt. And the air wasn't clean. Bits of fluff floated in it, and it smelled weird, too. Birds zipped through the air like hovertoys launched from tree limbs—were they even birds? He'd seen so few on Luna.

At least he was alone. A year ago, he would have hated not having anyone to goof around with or show off for. No coach, no team, no fans. Now he was grateful. Marta was watching out for him, always on the other end of a ping if anything went wrong. It was a relief not having to stay ultra-alert.

He pinged Marta.

How long do I have to stay in Paizuo?

Her face appeared again. She was shoveling noodles into her mouth with a pair of chopsticks. The sight of the food made his stomach heave.

At least two weeks. More if I can wrangle an extension. Ideally, I'd like you to stay until the tribunal decides your case.

Okay.

Two weeks. Fine. He'd keep doing what she said, within reason. Drinking water, yes. Slowing the bike down, no. He wasn't going to toil up the mountain like some slack-ass oldster.

Wasn't long before he regretted that decision. The nausea wouldn't be denied any longer. He shifted on the bike's saddle and hung his head over the edge of the guideway. His mouth prickled with saliva until his guts heaved, forcing what was left of his luxurious, hand-cooked Danzhai lunch—black fungus, eggplant, cucumbers, and garlic with pepper, pepper, and more pepper—up, out, and over into the green gulch below. The nausea eased.

When he got to the Paizuo landing stage, the guideway came to a dead end. He couldn't believe it. Just a ground-level platform with a bike rack on one side and a battery of cargo floats on the other. Zhang Lei had never even seen a landing stage with only one connection, not even in the bowels of Luna's smallest hab. Everywhere was interconnected. Not Paizuo, apparently.

He hooked his bike on the rack, shouldered his duffle bag, and wiped his mouth on his sleeve, flicking away a few stray pepper seeds. His lips burned.

I said you'd puke, Marta whispered. No visual this time, only a disembodied voice. *Bet you feel like shit.*

Yeah, but you look like shit.

It was the traditional Lunar reply. Marta laughed.

Don't pull that lip here, okay? You're a guest. Be polite.

He shifted his bag from one shoulder to the other. Nobody seemed to be watching, aside from Marta. Behind the trees, a few brown houses climbed the side of the mountain. Where was the village? A few people were visible through the trees, but otherwise, Paizuo was a wilderness—a noisy wilderness. Wind in the leaves, birds chirping, and buzzing—something coming up behind him.

Zhang Lei spun, fists raised. A cargo conveyor zipped up the guideway. It slid its payload onto a float and slotted itself into place on the underside of the landing stage. The float slowly meandered up a leafy path.

A hospitality fake showed him the way to the guest house, where he stumbled to his room, fell on top of the bed, and slept fourteen hours straight. If someone had wanted to kill him then, they easily could have. He wouldn't have cared.

The other three artists in the guest house were pampered oldsters from high-status habs. They made a big show of acting casual, but Zhang Lei caught each of them exchanging meaningful looks. They were probably pinging his ID to ogle his disable button, marveling at the label under it that said KILLER—FAIR GAME, and discussing him in whispers.

During lunch, Zhang Lei ignored them. Instead of joining their conversation, he watched a hygiene bot polish the floor.

"The wood bothered me at first," said Prajapati, gesturing with a beringed hand at the guest house's wooden walls, floor, and ceiling. She looked soft, her dark skin plush with fat and burnished with moisturizers. Her metadata identified her as a sculptor from Bangladesh Hell. "But organic materials are actually quite hygienic, if treated properly."

"I don't like the dirt," said Paul, an ancient watercolorist from Mars. "It's everywhere outside."

"It's not dirt, it's soil," said the sculptor. She picked a morsel of flesh out of the bubbling pot of fish soup in the middle of the table.

"People from the outplanet diaspora forget that soil is life," said Han Song, a 2D photographer from Beijing Hive.

"Yes, we've all been told that a thousand times," replied the watercolorist with a smile. "Earth thinks very well of itself. But I have to say, I like Paizuo. The Miao traditional lifestyle is extremely appealing."

A woman shuffled into the dining room bearing plates of egg dumplings and sweet millet cake. The oldsters smiled and thanked her profusely. The woman wore a wide silver torque around her neck, hung with tiny bells and charms. They tinkled as she arranged the dishes. She was slender, but the profile of her abdomen showed a huge tumor under her colorful tunic.

"What a waste of billable hours," the watercolorist said once the chef was gone. "Couldn't they task a bot with the kitchen-to-table supply chain? I know tradition is important to the Miao, but the human ability to carry plates is hardly going to die out."

The chef had tagged the food with detailed nutritional notes, and it said millet was good for digestive upset. After vomiting his Danzhai lunch yesterday, he couldn't face more peppers. But the millet cake was good—honey-sweet and crunchy. The egg dumplings were delicious, too. He could eat the whole plate.

Marta pinged him.

I thought you'd never wake up. Listen, don't worry about the other guests, okay? We've had them investigated. They're all nice, quiet, trustworthy people. They agreed not to ask too many questions.

He shoved another dumpling in his mouth. Zhang Lei knew he ought to be grateful but he wasn't. The three oldsters were getting something out of the deal, too. They would be able to tell stories about him for the rest of their lives. *I once shared accommodations with a murderer. Well, not a murderer, I suppose, not exactly, my dear, but a killer. No, I never asked him what happened but you should have seen the disable button on his ID. It said KILLER right under it. I couldn't help but stare.*

Zhang Lei finished the dumplings and claimed the rest of the millet cake. He left the table still chewing, and slammed the front door behind him.

What did you tell them about me? he asked Marta.

Not much. I said you weren't responsible for what happened and we're working to have the disable button removed.

I was responsible, though.

Zhang Lei, we've discussed this. Do you want to ping a peer counselor? Talk therapy is effective.

No. I hate talking.

The guest house was part of a trio of houses, fronted by a cabbage patch. Large birds—domestic poultry he guessed—pecked at the gravel walkway that led to the guest house's kitchen door. Nearby, a huge horned mammal was tethered in the shade, along with a large caged bird that stalked back and forth and shrieked.

Zhang Lei trudged toward a peak-roofed pavilion. The midday sun stood high over the valley, veiled by humid haze. Not at all hot, but in the unfamiliar atmosphere, sweat beaded on his scarred forearms.

The pavilion overlooked the terraced fields descending the valley and the hazy fleet of mountains on the horizon. No blue sky today. He might as well be in a near-Sun orbit greenhouse hab, deep in the eye of its dome, every sprout, bud, and bloom indexed and graphed. The locals probably used the same agricultural tech here. Each of the green-and-yellow plants in the terraces below was probably monitored by an agronomist up the mountain, watching microsensors buried in the soil and deploying mineral nutrition with pinpoint accuracy.

Zhang Lei pinged one of the plants. Nothing came back, not even an access denial. He tried pinging one of the farmers working far below, then a nearby tree. Still nothing. Frantic, he flung pings across the valley.

All of the Paizuo guest houses answered immediately. A map highlighted various routes up and down the valley. The guideway landing stage sent him the past two days of traffic history and offered average travel times to various down-slope destinations. A lazy stream of ID information flowed from the guest artists, thirty in total.

Several hazard warnings floated over their targets: *Watch for snakes. Beware of dog. Dangerous cliff.* But no pings from the locals, or any of the crops, equipment, or businesses. Not even from the wooden hand-truck upended over a pile of dirt at the side of the path. But no way this village ran everything data-free.

His pings summoned the hospitality fake. It hovered at his elbow, head inclined with a gently inquiring look.

"Why can't I get a pingback from anything here?" he demanded.

It gave Zhang Lei a generic smile. "Paizuo data streams are restricted to members of the Miao indigenous community."

"So I can't find out anything?" His face grew hot with anger. Stuck here for weeks or more, totally ignorant, unable to learn anything or find out how the village worked.

The fake nodded. "I'll be pleased to answer your questions if I'm able."

Zhang Lei wasn't in the mood for crèche-level games. He slapped it down, hard. The fake misted away, immediately replaced by Marta in full length. She had her fists on her hips and didn't look pleased.

Feeling a little aggressive, Zhang Lei? You didn't say two words to your fellow guests, and now you're getting testy with a fake.

I'm sorry, okay? Embarrassing. He should have controlled himself. *I hate this place.*

No, you don't. You're out of your element. Nothing here is any threat to you. She grinned. *Not unless you have a phobia of domestic animals.*

Hah, he grumbled.

Go for a walk. Do a little sketching. Get familiar with the village. There's lots to see, and it's all gorgeous. There's a reason why artists love Paizuo.

Okay. He booted up his viewcatcher. Marta gave him an approving nod and dissolved.

True, Paizuo was beautiful. From the pavilion, mountains thick with trees stretched sharp and steep over the valley, where green and yellow terraced fields stepped up and down the lower slopes, punctuated by small groups of wooden houses under tall trees. He framed the composition in his viewcatcher. It was perfect, pre-chewed—the whole reason the pavilion had been built there in the first place. The fang-like form of the tallest mountain clutched in the spiral fist of the golden mean. Nice.

Even though the view was prepackaged, framing it in his viewcatcher was satisfying. And what a relief to be able to do it openly. Back on Luna, he had to be careful not to get caught using the viewcatcher, or he'd get smacked by one of his teammates or screamed at by his coach. Zhang Lei was allowed to draw cartoons and caricatures, but everything else was a distraction from training and a waste of time and focus.

Total commitment to the game, that's what all coaches demanded.

"What do you love better, hockey or scribbling on little bits of paper?" Coach had demanded, and then smacked him on the back of the head when he hesitated.

"Hockey," he answered.

"Right. Don't forget it."

So he drew cartoons of his teammates, their rival teams, and stars from the premier leagues they all wanted to get drafted into. He got good. Fast. Accurate. In thirty seconds, he could toss off a sketch that got the whole team hooting. Coach liked it, said it was good for morale. But quick, sketchy work didn't satisfy. Neither did the digital-canvas painting he snuck past Coach on occasion, but both were better than nothing.

He padded down a trail to the first terrace, flipping his viewcatcher through its modes—thirds to notan to golden mean to phi grid—as he strode along the edge. The earthen berm bounding the terrace was less than a meter wide, and seemed to be made entirely of dirt. The next terrace was ten meters below on his left.

He blacked out edges of the view, widened the margins until nothing was visible outside his constantly expanding and contracting search for a composition. He swept back and forth across the landscape. Then he slipped and fell. The viewcatcher framed a close-up of green plants in brown water.

Zhang Lei lurched sideways, regaining his footing, the right leg of his pants wet to the knee and slimy with mud. He dismissed the viewcatcher and stared incredulously around him.

The matrix of the terraces was liquid, not soil. Water and mud. He'd seen it glinting between the greenery, but he hadn't realized it was water. And now he was covered in it.

A fleeting thought—*I'm going to die here*—easily dismissed. All he had to do was watch where he put his feet as he explored.

Paizuo wasn't what Zhang Lei expected. The village wasn't all one piece like ancient towns in crèche storybooks. It was spread thin, covering the whole valley, the houses clustered in groups under the trees and separated by fields and paddies. The Miao didn't build on flat or even sloping land—those areas seemed dedicated to crops. Instead, they chose the precipitous and rocky landscape for their multilevel wooden homes. Each house stood on stilts over the canted landscape, the weight of the structures leaning back on the mountainside. Livestock sheltered in the shade beneath, some tethered or penned, some roaming free.

Actual live animals, like the ones behind the guest house, and a lot of them. With humans living literally on top of them.

A deep voice knocked Zhang Lei out of his thoughts. Unfamiliar syllables. When he turned to look, the translation word balloon hung over the man's head:

"Hello, can I help you?"

No ID accessible, but the balloon was tagged with his name: Jen Dang. Not tall, but broad-shouldered and athletic, with skin deeply burnished by the sun and a wide, strong face. Old, but not an oldster.

Zhang Lei switched on his translation app.

"I arrived yesterday," Zhang Lei said. "Trying to get used to everything."

Jen Dang scanned the balloon overhead.

"Are the insects troubling you?"

"Insects?" Zhang Lei frowned and scanned the ground. "I haven't seen any yet."

"Right there." Jen Dang pointed at one of the fluttering creatures he had no name for.

"Oh, I thought insects lived on the ground. I'm from—" He almost said Luna but caught himself in time. "I've never been on Earth before. It's different."

"Most of our guests use seers to help them identify plants and animals. Paizuo is a biodiversity preserve, with thousands of different species."

"I'll do that, thanks."

Jen Dang fell silent. Zhang Lei could feel himself warming to the stranger. Lots of charisma and natural authority. He'd do well on Luna.

"The food is really good here," he said.

A shadow of a smile crossed Jen Dang's face.

"Jen Dla is my daughter. She's an experienced chef."

"I'm sorry," Zhang Lei said, and other man squinted at him. "I couldn't help but notice she's sick." He gestured vaguely in the region of his stomach.

Jen Dang shook his head. "You're a guest. There are lots of things guests can't understand. Would you like to see another?"

Two large baskets lay under a tree. Jen Dang plucked them from the ground and led Zhang Lei down a tree-lined path, the slope so extreme the route soon turned into uneven stairs, cut into the dirt and haphazardly incised with slabs of rock. Mammals grazed on either side, standing nearly on their hind legs while cropping the ground cover.

They descended five terrace levels before Zhang Lei's thighs started getting hot. Stairs were a good workout, mostly cardio but some leg strength, and uneven steps were good balance training, too. For a moment he lost himself in the rhythm of their rapid descent. It was enjoyable. He could run the stairs in morning and evening before doing his squats and lunges—but then he remembered. He wasn't an athlete anymore. And with the disable button on his ID labeling him a killer, nobody in Danzhai, Miao or guest, needed to wonder what he was training for, or if he was chasing someone.

He slowed, letting the distance widen between himself and the farmer. If someone got worried and hit the button, he'd roll right down the mountain.

Jen Dang shucked his shoes and rolled up his trouser legs as he waited for Zhang Lei at one of the lower terraces.

"Many guests are squeamish of the rice paddies, but it's only water and mud," he said when Zhang Lei joined him. "And worms. Bugs of course. A few snakes. And fish." He hefted the large basket. It was bottomless—an open, woven cylinder.

"Not a problem." Zhang Lei pulled off his shoes, but didn't roll up his pant legs. One was still damp. The other might as well get wet, too.

Jen Dang handed him the smaller basket and waded into the sodden paddy, bottomless basket clutched in both hands.

"Step between the rice plants, never on them. Try not to stir up too much mud, or you can't see the fish."

Jen Dang demonstrated, moving slowly and looking at the water through the basket. Zhang Lei followed. The mud was cool. It squelched through his toes.

"Use the basket to shade the water's surface," the farmer said. "Look for movement. A flash of scales or the flick of a tail."

As Zhang Lei followed the farmer through the paddy, he took care to keep his feet away from the knee-high rice plants. Each one was topped by knobby spikes—the grain portion of the crop, he assumed. Some of the grain was coated with a milky substance, and some was turning yellow.

Jen Dang plunged the bottomless basket in the water and said, "Come look."

A fish was trapped inside. Jen Dang reached into the water and flipped it into Zhang Lei's basket. It struggled, thrashing.

"That's one, we need six. You catch the rest."

Zhang Lei made several tries before he trapped a fish large enough to meet Jan Dang's standards. Catching the rest took a full hour. The sky cleared and turned Earth-blue. The older man betrayed no trace of impatience, even though it was a ridiculous expenditure of effort to procure basic foodstuffs when a nutritional extruder could feed hundreds of people an hour, with personalized flavor and texture profiles and optimal nutrition.

When they finished, Zhang Lei's eyes ached from squinting against the flare of sun on water. He wiped his fish-slick hands on his pants and followed the farmer up the stairs.

"Why do you do this?" he asked.

Jen Dang stopped and eyed the word balloon over Zhang Lei's head.

"Stubbornness. That's what my wife says. She's a orthopedic surgeon, takes care of all the Miao in Danzhai county. She won't farm. Says her hands are meant for higher things. She loves to cook, though. She taught all our daughters."

"But why do manual labor when you could use bots?"

"We use some, but we're not dependent on them. If we don't do the work, who will?"

"Nobody."

"Then nobody will know how to do it. All traditional skills and knowledge will be lost, along with our language, stories, songs—everything that makes us Miao. We do it to survive."

"You could write it down."

Jen Dang laughed. He lifted the fish basket to his shoulder and ran up the stairs two at a time. His word balloon blossomed behind him.

"Some things can only be mastered with constant practice."

That was true. Nobody could learn to play hockey by watching a doc. Or learn to draw or paint without actually doing it.

An insect landed on a nearby plant. Its wide, delicate wings had eyelike patterns in shades of gold and copper. Zhang Lei framed it in his viewcatcher, then panned up to include the mountains in the composition. Gold wings and green slopes, copper eyes and blue sky. Perfect.

Another insect hung in the sky, hovering motionless, shaped like a half circle and very faint. Zhang Lei stared for a whole minute before realizing what he was looking at.

The moon. Luna itself. The home of everything he knew, and everyone who wanted to hurt him. Watching.

Over the next week, the moon turned its back on him, retreating through its last quarter to a thinning sickle. In the morning, when he ventured onto the guest house's porch for a stretch, there it was, lurking behind the boughs of a fir tree, half-hidden behind mountain peaks, or veiled in humid haze to the east. Sometimes it hid on the other side of the globe. Then the next time he looked, it was right overhead, staring at him.

Night was the worst. The lights of the habs glared from the dark lunar surface aside the waning crescent—the curved sickle of Purovsk, the oval of Olenyok, the diamond pinpoint of Bratsk, the five-pointed star of Harbin.

A few years back, an investment group had tried to float a proposal to build a new hab on Mare Insularum, its lights outlining a back-turned fist with an extended middle finger. Zhang Lei and his teammates had worn the proposed hab pattern on their gym shirts for a few months, the finger mocked up extra large on a dark moon, telling Earth and all its inhabitants what Lunites thought of them.

He could stay inside at night, but he couldn't hide from the moon during the day. It watched him with a sideways smile. *We see you—we're coming to get you.*

He tried not to think about it, and concentrated on finding compositions with his viewcatcher. He made sketches and studies, and looked up plants and animals with his seer, and tried to learn their names. When he ran into artists from the other guest houses, they were friendly enough, but all much older than him.

At night, he worked on studies and small canvases in his room, door closed and windows dark. They were disasters: muddy greens, lifeless brushwork, flat compositions. He tried all the tricks he'd learned in the crèche—glazing, underpainting, overpainting, scraping with a palette knife, dry brush, but nothing worked.

Why don't you try some familiar subjects? Marta suggested. *Limber up first, then branch out into new things.*

If you say so.

He was so frustrated he'd try anything. He lugged his easel and kit up to the guest house's communal studio and set up in his own corner of the work space.

"I was beginning to think we'd never see you up here," said Paul. "Welcome."

"The light's especially good in the afternoon," said Prajapati.

Han Song paused his hands over his work surface for a moment and nodded.

Nothing motivated Zhang Lei like competition. He would destroy the watercolorist with his superior command of light and shadow, teach the sculptor about form, show the photographer how to compose a scene.

His old viewcatcher compositions and stealthily-made reference sketches were gone forever, so he worked from memory. He attacked the canvas with his entire arsenal, blocking out a low-angle view of Mons Hadley and the shining towers of Sklad, with the hab's vast hockey arena in the foreground under a gleaming crystal dome. The view might be three hundred and eighty thousand kilometers away, but it lay at his fingertips, and he created it anew every time he closed his eyes.

The paint leapt to Zhang Lei's brush, clung to the canvas, spread thin and lean and true exactly where it should, the way it should, creating the effects he intended. After a week of flailing with sappy greens and sloppy, organic shapes, he finally had a canvas under control. He worked late, muttering good night to the other artists without raising his eyes from his work. When dawn stretched its fingers through the studio's high windows, the painting was done—complete with a livid crimson stain spreading under the arena's crystal dome.

He didn't remember deciding to paint blood on the ice, or putting crimson on his palette. But the color belonged there. It was the truth. It showed what he did.

Zhang Lei lowered himself to the floor, leaned his back against the wall with his elbows on his knees, and rested his head in his hands. He pinged Marta. She blinked blearily at him for a few seconds, her eyes swollen with sleep. He pointed at the canvas.

Have any of the other artists seen this? she whispered.

I don't know. I don't think so.

It's important they don't. Okay? Do you understand why?

Because people are looking for me.

Not only that. She scrubbed her eyes with the heels of her hands. *The Lunite ambassador is trying to block your immigration application. She made an official information request. If the media gets interested we'll have to move you, fast. And yes, people are searching. Three teams of Lunite brawlers have been skipping all over the planet, asking questions. They found someone in Sudbury Hell who remembers you getting on a skip bound for Chongqing Hive. That's too close for comfort.*

I can destroy the canvas, he said, voice flat and scraped clean of emotion. It was the first real painting he'd done since he left the crèche. But he couldn't look at it. When he did, his flesh crawled.

No. Don't do that. Hide it.

He nodded. *It's a decent painting.*

Yeah. Not bad. You worked out the kinks.

He knocked his head against the wall behind him. Wood was harder than it looked. He swung his head harder.

Stop that.

There's no point, Marta. Those brawlers are going to find me.

No, they won't. And chances are good the tribunal will rule in your favor. We have to be patient.

Even if I get to live in Beijing, people will still find out what I did.

They'll assume you had no choice. Everyone knows Luna is the most dangerous place in the solar system.

I did have a choice—

Marta interrupted. *It was a mistake. An accident. It could happen to any hockey player.*

I aimed for Dorgon's neck.

You did what you were taught, and so did Dorgon. Playing hockey isn't the only way to die on Luna. If you live in a place where getting killed is accepted as a possible outcome, then you also accept that you might become a killer.

But we don't understand what it means.

No. Marta looked sad. *No, we don't.*

The day after he'd killed Dorgon, Zhang Lei's team hauled him to a surgeon. Twenty minutes was all it took to install the noose around his carotid artery, then two minutes to connect the disable button and process the change to his ID. His teammates were as gentle as they could be. When it was all done, the team's enforcer clasped Zhang Lei's shoulder in a meaty hand.

"We test it now," Korchenko said, and Zhang Lei had gone down like a slab of meat.

When he woke, his friends looked concerned, sympathetic, even a little regretful.

That attitude didn't last long. After the surgery, the team traveled to a game in Surgut. Zhang Lei's disable button was line-of-sight. Anyone who could see it could trigger it. He passed out five times along the way, and spent most of the game slumped on the bench, head lolling, his biom working hard to keep him from brain damage. His teammates had to carry him home.

For a few weeks, they treated him like a mascot, hauling him from residence to practice rink to arena and back again. They soon tired of it and began leaving him behind. The first time he went out alone he came back on a cargo float, with a shattered jaw and boot-print-shaped bruises on his gut. That was okay. He figured he deserved it.

Then one night after an embarrassing loss, the team began hitting the button for fun. First Korchenko, as a joke. Then the others. Didn't take long for Zhang Lei to become their new punching bag. So he ran. Hid out in Sklad's lower levels, pulling temporary privacy veils over his ID every fifteen minutes to keep the team from tracking him. When they were busy at the arena warming up for a game, he bolted for Harbin.

He passed out once on the way to the nearest intra-hab connector, but the brawler who hit his disable button was old and drunk. Zhang

Lei collected a few kicks to the ribs and one to the balls before the drunk staggered off. Nobody else took the opportunity to get their licks in, but nobody helped him, either.

Boarding the connector, he got lucky. A crèche manager was transferring four squalling newborns, and the crib's noise-dampening tech was broken. The pod emptied out—just him and the crèche manager. She ignored him all the way to Harbin. He kept his distance, but when they got to their destination, he followed her into the bowels of the hab. She was busy with the babies and didn't notice at first. But when he joined her in an elevator, she got scared.

"What do you want?" she demanded, her voice high with tension.

He tried to explain, but she was terrified. That big red label on his button—KILLER—FAIR GAME—didn't fill people with confidence in his character. She hit the button hard, several times. He spent an hour on the floor of the elevator, riding from level to level, and came to with internal bleeding, a cracked ocular orbit, three broken ribs, and a vicious bite mark on his left buttock.

He limped down to the lowest level, where they put the crèches, and found his old crèche manager. She was gray, stooped, and much more frail than he remembered.

"Zhang Lei." She put a gentle palm on his head—the only place that didn't hurt. "I was your first cuddler. I decanted you myself. I won't let anyone hurt you."

If he cried then, he never admitted it.

Zhang Lei watched Jen Dla carry a pot of soup into the dining room. She moved awkwardly, shifting her balance around that bulbous gut. He couldn't understand it. Why hadn't she had an operation to remove the tumor? Her mother was even a surgeon.

Terminal, he guessed, and then realized he'd been staring.

Jen Dla nestled the pot on the stove in the middle of the table, and lit the flame. He caught the chef's eye as she adjusted the temperature of the burner.

"Your father must be an important man here in Paizuo," he said.

Jen Dla laughed.

"He certainly thinks so." She laid her hand on the embroidered blouse draped over her bulging abdomen. "Fathers get more self-important with every new grandchild."

She tapped her finger on her stomach. Zhang Lei sat back in his chair, abruptly. She wasn't sick, but pregnant—actually bearing a child.

"Are all Miao children body-birthed?" he blurted.

She looked a little offended. "Miao who choose to live in Paizuo generally like to follow tradition."

Abrupt questions leapt behind his teeth—*does it hurt, are you frightened*—but her expression was forbidding.

"Congratulations," he said. She smiled and returned to her kitchen.

After talking to Marta, he'd taken the painting down to his room and hidden it under the bed, then collapsed into dream-clouded sleep. The arena at Sklad, deserted, the vast spread of ice all his own. The blades of his skates cut the surface as he built speed, gathered himself, and launched into a quad, spinning through the air so fast the flesh of his face pulled away and snapped back into place on landing. He jumped, spun, jumped again.

Dreams of power and joy, ruined on waking. He'd pulled the painting from under his bed and hid it behind the sofa in the guest house lounge.

Jen Dla's soup began to bubble. Tomatoes bobbed in the sour rice broth. Zhang Lei watched the fish turn opaque as it cooked, then pinged one word at the three artists upstairs—*lunch*. They clattered down.

"Looked like you were having a productive session yesterday," Prajapati said. "Good to see."

"Don't stop the flow," Han Song added.

Paul grinned. "Nothing artists love more than giving unwanted advice."

"It's called encouragement," said Prajapati. "And it's especially important for young artists."

"Young competitors, you mean."

"I don't see it that way." She turned to Zhang Lei. "Do you?"

All three artists watched him expectantly. Zhang Lei stared at his hands resting on the wooden tabletop. He'd forgotten to roll down his sleeves. His forearms were exposed, the scarred skin dotted with pigment. He put his hands in his lap.

"I think the fish is ready," he said.

After lunch, while exploring for new compositions, he found Jen Dang behind the guest house. The water buffalo—one of the first creatures he'd looked up on his seer—was tethered to a post by a loop of rope through its nose. It was huge, lavishly muscled, and heavy, with ridged, back-curving horns, but it stood placidly as Jen Dang examined its hooves.

"Stay back," Jen Dang said. "Water buffalo aren't as friendly as they look. He's not a pet."

"Yeah, I know," said Zhang Lei. When he'd sketched the water buffalo, a stern warning had popped into his eye: *Do not approach. Will trample, gouge, and kick.*

He lifted his viewcatcher and captured a composition: Jen Dang stooping with his back turned to the water buffalo, drawing its massive hindquarter between his own legs and trapping the hoof between his knees.

"All he has to do is back up, and you'll get squashed," said Zhang Lei.

"He knows me." Jen Dang dropped the hoof and patted the animal's rump. "And he knows the best part of his day is about to begin."

The farmer untied the rope from the post and led the animal up the narrow trail behind the houses. Zhang Lei followed. A bird stalked from between the trees, its red, gold, and blue body trailing long, spotted brown tail feathers. His seer tagged it: *Golden Pheasant*, followed by a symbol that meant *major symbolic and cultural importance to the indigenous people at this geographical location*. Which was no different from most of the plants and animals the seer had identified.

"So, I've been using a seer," he said, as if his rice paddy conversation with Jen Dang had happened that morning instead of days ago. "It doesn't explain anything. Why is every butterfly important to Miao but not the flies? Why one species of bee but not the other?"

"The butterfly is our mother," Jen Dang said.

"No, it's not. That's ridiculous."

"I might ask you who your mother is, if I were young and rude, and didn't know better."

"I don't have a mother. I was detanked."

"That means you're the product of genetic advection, from a tightly edited stream of genetic material subscribed to by your crèche. How is that less strange than having a butterfly mother?"

"Is the butterfly thing a metaphor?"

Jen Dang glanced over his shoulder, his gaze cold. "If you like."

The water buffalo lipped the tail of Jen Dang's shirt. He tapped its nose with the palm of his hand to warn it off. The trail widened as it began to climb a high ridge. The water buffalo was heavy but strong. It heaved itself up the slope, like a boulder rolling uphill. Jen Dang ran alongside to keep pace, so Zhang Lei ran after. The exertion felt good, scrambling uphill against the full one-point-zero, with two workout partners. So what if one of them was an animal? Zhang Lei would take what he could get.

When the trail widened, he took the chance to sprint ahead. He made it to the top of the ridge a full ten seconds before the water buffalo. Jen Dang looked him up and down.

"Not bad. Most guests are slow."

Zhang Lei grinned. "I train in the dubs."

"Dubs?"

"Double Earth-normal gravity. You know. For strength."

"I never would have guessed."

"I know," Zhang Lei said eagerly. "I look bottom-heavy, right? Narrow above a wide butt and thick legs. That's what makes me a good skater."

Shut up, Marta hissed in his ear. But he couldn't stop. Finally a real conversation.

"I train for optimal upper body flexibility, like all center forward play—"

One twinge in his throat, that's all it took to send Zhang Lei plummeting to the ground. He twisted and rolled when he hit the dirt—away from the edge of the hill, and then the world faded to mist.

Zhang Lei clawed his way to consciousness.

You're fine, you're fine, nobody's touched you.

Okay, he mumbled.

You've only been down five minutes, Marta added. *Tell him you have a seizure disorder and your neurologist is fine-tuning your treatment protocol. Say it.*

Zhang Lei struggled to focus. His eyelids fluttered as he tried to form the words.

"I get seizures." He licked his lips. "Doc's working on it."

Jen Dang said something. Zhang Lei forced his eyes to stay open. He was collapsed on his side, cheek pressed to the dirt. Three ants crawled not ten centimeters from his eye. He flopped onto his back to read the farmer's word balloon.

"Your medical advisory said it wasn't an emergency, and I shouldn't touch you." Behind Jen Dang, the water buffalo cast a lazy brown eye over him and shook its head.

Tell him you'll be fine, Marta demanded. *Ask him not to mention it to anyone.*

"I'm fine." Zhang Lei pushed himself onto his elbows, then to his knees. "Don't talk about this, okay?"

The farmer looked dubious. He gathered the water buffalo's lead rope. "I'll walk you back to the studio."

"No." Zhang Lei jumped to his feet. "There's nothing wrong with me. It won't happen again."

Better not, Marta grumbled.

Zhang Lei led the way up the trail. Jen Dang followed. The water buffalo wasn't dawdling anymore, it was moving fast, nearly trotting. The track converged on a single-lane paved road, which snaked up the valley in a series of switchbacks. They were higher now, the guest houses far below, and everywhere, rice terraces brimmed with ripening grain yellow as the sun. He could paint those terraces with slabs of cadmium yellow. Maybe he would.

"Which way?"

Zhang Lei needn't have asked. The water buffalo turned onto the road and trundled uphill. Before long, the slope gentled. Houses lined the road, with gardens and rice paddies behind. The road ended at a circular courtyard patterned with dark and light stones and half-bounded by a stream. At the far end, a footbridge arched over the water, leading to more houses beyond.

The animal's tail switched back and forth. It trotted toward the water, splayed hooves clopping on the courtyard's patterned surface. A hygiene sweeper darted out of its path. At the stream's edge, where the courtyard's stone patterns gave way to large, dark slabs, the water buffalo paused, lowered its head, and stepped into the water.

A man called out from one of the houses across the bridge. Jen Dang shouted a reply. No word balloon appeared.

Jen Dang offered the lead rope to Zhang Lei.

"He'll stay in the water. I'll only be a few minutes."

Zhang Lei leaned on the bridge railings, flipping the rope to keep it from tangling in the animal's horns as it luxuriated in the water below. The stream wasn't deep, only a meter or so, but the beast lay on its side and rolled, keeping its white beard, eyes, and horns above water.

When Jen Dang returned, the water buffalo was scratching its long, drooping ear on a half-submerged rock. Zhang Lei kept the rope.

"It's fun," he said. "Best part of my day, too."

The farmer sauntered across the courtyard and joined a pair of friends working in the shade of a mulberry tree.

Zhang Lei composed a series of canvases. The water buffalo with its eyelids lowered in pleasure, lips parted to reveal a gleaming row of bottom teeth. Three women in bright blue blouses weaving in an open workshop, their silver torques flashing. A man in deep indigo embroidered with pink and silver diamonds, sorting through a table piled with feathers. Jen Dang leaning on a low stone wall, deep in conversation with two friends using gleaming axes to chop lengths of bamboo. A white-haired woman in an apron stirring a barrel of viscous liquid with a wooden paddle. A battery of pink-cheeked, scrubbed children racing across the courtyard as a golden pheasant stalked in the opposite direction. A row of cabbages beside the road. Herbs clinging to a slate outcropping. A dragonfly skipping over the water. The tallest peak puncturing the western horizon like a fang on the underjaw of a huge beast.

Aesthetically pleasing, peaceful, picturesque. But all communities had tensions and contradictions. Only a Miao could identify the deeper meaning in these scenes. Only a great artist could paint the picturesque and make it important. He wasn't Miao and he was no great artist. Could he capture the water buffalo's expression of ecstasy as it pawed the water? Not likely. But he could paint the mountain. Nothing more banal than another mountain view. But he loved that unnamed peak. He'd loved Mons Hadley, too.

Jen Dang waved. A word balloon blossomed over his head: *Let's go.*

He jiggled the rope. The water buffalo ignored him. He flapped it, then gave the gentlest of tugs. The buffalo snorted and heaved itself out of the water. It stood there dripping for a moment, then its skin shivered. It lowered its head, shaking its great bulk and coating Zhang Lei in a local rainstorm.

Zhang Lei wiped his face on his sleeve. The men were still laughing when he joined them. Nothing more fun than watching a rookie fall on his ass.

Jen Dang was still chatting. Zhang Lei waited nearby, in the shade of a house. Along the wall was a metal cage much like the one behind the guest house. A rooster stalked back and forth, its face, comb, and wattle bright red, its bare breast and scraggly back caked with clean, healing sores. It stared at Zhang Lei with a malevolent orange eye, lifted one fiercely-taloned yellow leg, and flipped its water dish.

"Stupid bird," Zhang Lei muttered.

Around the corner was another cage, another rooster in similar condition, its comb sliced in dangling pieces. When it screamed—raucous, belligerent—the other bird answered. Zhang Lei knew an exchange of challenges when he heard it.

"Are these fighting cocks?" he asked when Jen Dang joined him.

"You don't have them on Luna?" he answered.

Shit, whispered Marta. *Tell him you're from the Sol Belt. You've never been to Luna.*

Why don't you hit my disable button again? Load me on a cargo float and stick me in a hole somewhere? Or better yet—a cage. Evict one of the birds and get me my own dish of water.

I might have to do that. Listen kid, it's never been more important for you to be discreet.

Why? Are they coming for me?

Silence.

They are, aren't they? Answer me.

A Lunite team tracked you to the Danzhai roadhouse, but don't worry. We've got people on the ground, planting rumors to lure them to Guiyang. Even if they don't take the bait, Danzhai County has lots of towns and villages. You're still safe.

"I'm from the Sol Belt," he told Jen Dang. "I've never been to Luna."

The farmer didn't look convinced.

Zhang Lei's hand stole up to his throat. Under his jaw, where his pulse pounded, the hard mass of the noose waited to choke off his life.

When Zhang Lei got back to the studio, the other three artists were upstairs. He shoved the sofa aside. The painting leaned against the wall, facing out, a layer of breathable sealant protecting the drying oil paint. He was sure he'd turned it to face the wall, but apparently not. It didn't really matter. He wanted it gone.

He sprayed the canvas with another layer of sealant, trying not to look at the thick wet bloody gleam on the arena's ice. He wrapped it in two layers of black polymer sheeting, and requested a cargo wrap to meet him at the guideway landing stage.

When he got there, the area was packed with Miao arriving on sliders and bikes, whole families crowded onto multi-seat units, laughing and talking. He edged his way to the cargo drop, slid the cargo wrap around it, addressed it to Marta, and shoved the painting inside the conveyor. Done. He'd never have to think about it again.

The Miao were on holiday. Women wore their blue blouses with short skirts trailing with long, flapping ribbons, or ankle-length red and blue dresses. All the women's clothing was dense with colorful embroidery and tinkling with silver, and all wore their silver torques. The younger women pierced their topknots with flowers. Mothers and grandmothers layered their torques with necklaces, and wore tall silver headdresses crowned with slender, curving horns. Silver everywhere—charms in the shape of flowers, bells, fish, and butterflies dangled from their jewelry, sleeves, sashes, and hems.

They were, in a word, gorgeous. Happy-laughing, leading children, carrying babies, holding hands with their friends, and among them, men of all ages in embroidered black, blue, and indigo. The men were also happy, also laughing, also embracing their friends, helping their children and elders. But the young women—ah. They caught his eye.

Zhang Lei retreated to the side of a corn patch, capturing compositions while watching the steady flow of arrivals. Some pinged for mobility assistance, and rode float chairs up the road, but most walked. Some eschewed the road, and ran uphill toward the guest house, making for the steep shortcut up the ridge. Zhang Lei followed.

Paul, Prajapati, and Han Song watched from the studio porch. Zhang Lei joined them.

"Jen Dla told me we can go watch the festival after supper," Prajapati said. "It's called Setting Free Your Daughter, or something like that."

"Setting them free from what?" asked Han Song.

Six young women ran toward them, through Jen Dla's cabbage patch.

"Family control, I would imagine," Paul answered.

The girls didn't even glance up. At home, he never had to work to get a girl's attention—nobody on the team did. Unless coach called a ban for training reasons, sex was on offer everywhere he looked. Here, he might as well be invisible. But then, he hadn't exactly been making himself available. If the girls were being set free, and he was in the right place at the right time, maybe one of them would land in his lap. All he had to do was get them to notice him.

"I'm going to the festival," Zhang Lei said.

"I'll go too," said Han Song. "I haven't done enough exploring."

"We'll all go," said Prajapati. Paul nodded.

After Jen Dla served them an early supper, Zhang Lei led the oldsters up the winding road to the village center. They admired the views from every switchback as if they hadn't already had a week to explore, and examined every clump of flowers as if Paizuo wasn't one big flower garden. Guests from the other studios joined them, which made the whole group even slower.

Zhang Lei was tempted to leave them all behind, run to the village center and see if the girls had been set free yet. He jogged up a few switchbacks, and then thought the better of it. Even the most adventurous girl would flee from a lone man bearing a disable button labeled KILLER. If he wanted someone to take a chance on trusting him, he'd better stick with the group.

Zhang Lei sat on a boulder at the side of the road and waited for the oldsters to catch up. They weren't bad people. All three were kind and clever in their own ways. And patient. He'd been unfriendly but they hadn't taken offence.

"We should really walk faster," Prajapati told the other two when they caught up. "We don't want Zhang Lei to miss his chance with the girls."

Zhang Lei grinned. "I could ping you a cargo float."

She laughed and took his arm.

The roadside floating lights winked on, turning their route into a tunnel of light snaking up the mountainside. When they got to the village center, night had fallen. The courtyard was lit with flaming torches and in the middle of the crowd, a bonfire blazed, sending up a column of sparks to search the sky. Faces flickered with shadows. Silver glinted and gleamed. Laughter pealed. A singer wailed.

"I don't know when I last smelled something burning," said Han Song.

"Is that what the stench is?" asked Paul.

"Wood smoke is the most beautiful scent," said Prajapati. "Primal."

Most of the guests stayed on the courtyard's edge. They joined a group under the mulberry tree, a gender-free triad of performance artists from Cusco Hab. Zhang Lei had seen them around the village. They always looked like they were in a meeting—heads down, conferring, arguing, making notes.

"Have the daughters been set free yet?" Han Song quipped. "Asking for a friend."

The triad laughed.

"Apparently it's only one daughter, and no, the ceremony hasn't begun yet," said Aiko, the tallest of the three.

"Just one girl?" Zhang Lei said. "Then what's the point?"

"Shakespeare! One performer, one night only. The complete works." Aiko was obviously joking but their face was perfectly sober.

Prajapati grinned. "Don't tease the boy."

Another pair of artists joined them, a cellist from Zurich and an opera singer from Hokkaido. They seemed to know more about the festival than anyone else.

"We won't catch much of the performance unless the girl throws the switch on her translation balloon," the cellist said in a low voice. "The one last year didn't."

"Someone told me they translate in Kala, for the tourists visiting from Danzhai Wanda Village," said Aiko.

"Paizuo is more traditional than Kala. Which is why we come here." The cellist shaded her eyes against the torches' flare and scanned the crowd.

"It's better they don't translate," the opera singer said. "What the girl says won't make sense if you don't know the context. It's more meaningful to watch the reactions of the Miao."

With so many people in the square, Zhang Lei could only catch glimpses of the action. He put his viewcatcher on full extension, sent it a meter overhead, and switched its mode to low lux. Much better. The musicians were at the far end of the courtyard, near the bridge, playing drums and tall, upright bamboo flutes. The singer stood with them, wearing her silver headdress like a crown. Jen Dang and his family didn't seem to be around. But he spotted the girl—the one who was being set free. She was alone. No friends, no fussing parents, no little siblings hanging on her arms.

She wore hoops of silver chain around her torque, a blue blouse and short black skirt embroidered with butterflies, and a woven sash around her waist. A deep red flower pierced her topknot. Her hands rested at her sides. She didn't pick at her nails or play with her jewelry like Lunite girls. She looked prepared, like a goalie in a crease, waiting for the game to begin.

He zoomed in on her face. His age or a little younger. Pretty, like all the Miao girls. Tough, too. What would a girl like her think of him?

Not much, he suspected.

The music stopped, the crowd hushed. The girl's lips thinned in concentration. She stepped toward the bonfire and the circle of elders welcomed her into their arms. No drums this time, no bamboo flutes, no practiced wail from a powerful throat. The elders sang softly, their song a hum in the night, drowning under the buzz of the cicadas and crickets.

Near the artists at the back of the crowd stood a mother with a baby clutched to her chest. She wore little silver, and looked upset.

"Poor thing," said Prajapati.

The woman scowled at her and made a hushing motion.

Zhang Lei waited for something to happen, some reason why the Miao were paying such close attention. The girl wasn't doing anything, just standing in the circle of softly singing elders, eyes closed, face tight with concentration. Maybe nothing would happen—that was the point? Perhaps it was a test of her patience. It certainly was a test of his.

As he was considering sneaking away, the girl began singing along. Her voice was high, with an eerie overtone that pierced the sky. She sang higher and higher, drowning out the elders' voices. The Miao were rapt, breathless. When she spoke—loud as if amplified—the crowd exhaled a collective sigh of wonder.

"No translation balloon," Aiko breathed. "Damn."

Zhang Lei expected the crying mother to turn and scold them again, but she was pushing through the crowd, sobbing and holding her baby out like an offering.

"Must be her dead husband," said the cellist, quietly. "You see? They set the girl's soul free to visit the spirits, and now she's bringing messages back."

"Messages?" said Zhang Lei. "What kind of messages?"

"Every kind. Instructions. Admonitions. Warnings. Blessings. What kind of messages would you send from beyond if you could?"

"I don't know, maybe something the girl could easily guess?" said Han Song.

"Hush," said Prajapati. "This is serious."

It was serious. Zhang Lei didn't even have to look up to know the new moon was watching him, the lights of its habs inscribed like a curse on the sunless black disc punched through the middle of the Milky Way.

On Luna, hockey was a blood sport. Lunar hockey was played at one-sixth gravity on a curved surface, with a Stefoff field to keep the puck low and snap players back to the ice. One of the major defensive moves was to disable the other team's players. Clubbing with weighted carbon fiber hockey sticks resulted in a penalty, though all referees were selectively blind. Slashing with skate blades, however, was a power move. An overdominant team could cut their way through their opponents' starting lineup, into the benched players and fourth-rates, and by the end of the fourth quarter stage an assault on an undefended goalie.

Deaths were rare. Heads, legs, torsos, and groins were armored. Arms and throats were not. Medical bots hovered over the ice, ready to swoop in for first response, but rookies from the crèches quickly picked up scars, even playing in the recreational leagues. Anyone who remained unscarred was either a goalie or a coward.

Zhang Lei's crèche manager had tried to do right by him, direct his talents so he'd have choices when he left the crèche. She nurtured his talent for drawing and painting as much as possible. But she was practical, too. Luna had far more professional hockey teams than artist collectives. All her children were on skates as soon as they could walk.

With powerful legs and a low center of gravity, Zhang Lei could take a hit and keep his speed. He could jump, spin, and kick. He could slice an opposing defenseman's brachial artery, drag his stick through the spurting blood, and spray the goalie as he slid the puck into the net. The fans loved him for it. His teammates too.

It made him a target, though. He spent more time on the bench than anyone else on the team, healing wounds on his forearms. No matter. The downtime gave him the opportunity to perfect the rarest of plays—jump and spin high enough to slice a blade through an opponent's throat. He practiced it, talked about it, drew cartoons of it. He gave up goals attempting it, which got him a faceful of spittle whenever Coach chewed him out.

Then finally he did it.

Dorgon wasn't even Zhang Lei's favorite proposed target. He was just a young, heavy-duty defenseman with a loud mouth who wasn't scared of Zhang Lei's flying blades.

He should have been.

Dorgon bled out in ten seconds. The medbot wrapped him in a life support bubble and attempted a transfusion right there on the ice, but stumbled over the thick scars on the defenseman's arms. When it searched for alternate access, Dorgon's coach was too busy screaming at Zhang Lei to flip the master toggle on his player's armor.

Whose fault was it, then, that Dorgon died?

"Your fault, Zhang Lei," the Miao girl said. "You opened a mouth in my throat and my whole life came pouring out."

She pointed to him, standing under the mulberry tree with the other guests. Heads turned. He should have ran but he was frozen, breathless as if in a vacuum. He might have collapsed without the tree trunk behind him.

Marta? he whispered. *Help.*

No answer. Prajapati grabbed his arm.

"Ignore her, it's a trick," she said. And then louder: "That's not funny."

The crowd parted to allow the girl a clear sight of him.

"There's nowhere you can go that I won't follow. I'm inside your mattress when you sleep. Behind the door of your room, inside the closet. When you painted the Sklad arena, who do you think put the blood on the canvas? It was me."

She raised her fists and swung them toward him, as if shooting a puck with a phantom hockey stick.

"You're fair game."

The girl's head snapped back. She coughed once, and began speaking her native language again. The crowd turned away.

Marta? Answer me.

Prajapati tugged on his sleeve. "It's late. Walk me home. We'll take the shortcut."

She took his arm again, pretending to need it for balance on the rocky path, but in truth she was holding him up. Han Song and Paul trailed behind, talking in low voices.

Marta? Marta!

She answered before they got to top of the ridge.

Sorry, kid. I was in a closed-session meeting. Total privacy veil.

Are they coming for me?

What? No. Is there a problem in Paizuo?

Zhang Lei groaned. Prajapati looked at him sharply. Worry lines creased her plump face.

They know who I am. What I did.

Who knows?

Everyone. And all their relatives. From all over. Dorgon told them.

That's impossible.

He grabbed his viewcatcher, pinched off the last ten minutes of data, and fired it to her.

Watch this.

The path descending the ridge was treacherous, lit by nothing but stars. If he'd been alone, Zhang Lei would have ran down the ridge. If he fell and broke his neck, he deserved it. But the oldsters needed his help.

He took Prajapati's hand—warm, dry, strong—and used the fill flash on his viewcatcher to light each step while Han Song shone the brighter light from his camera down the trail. The two oldster men helped steady each other, Paul's hand on the photographer's shoulder. When Han Song slipped, Paul caught him by the elbow.

Yeah, okay, Marta whispered. *Someone figured out who you are and told the girl. I'll talk to the security team. Don't do anything stupid, okay? We're on this.*

When they got to the studio, Paul fetched a bottle of whiskey from his room. He poured four glasses and handed the largest one to Zhang Lei.

"I found the news feed from Luna a couple days ago," Paul said. "But I didn't tell anyone."

"I found the painting," said Prajapati. "I wasn't looking for it, but the sofa was in the wrong place. I showed it to Paul and Han Song. It's effective work, Zhang Lei. Palpable anguish."

"If you want to keep something private," said Han Song, "don't put it in the common areas."

"None of us told anyone," Prajapati added.

"So, how did the story get to the Miao girl?" Paul asked. The other two oldsters shook their heads.

"Jen Dla?" Han Song ventured.

"I'll ask her in the morning." Prajapati patted Zhang Lei's knee. "Try to get some sleep."

The whiskey burned Zhang Lei's throat and filled his sinuses with the scent of bonfire. *What kind of messages would you send from beyond if you could?* Vengeance. Dorgon had watched and waited for his opportunity. The news would travel fast. Brawler teams were searching the county for him.

Zhang Lei poured the rest of the whiskey down his throat.

"When they come for me, keep hitting my disable button," he said.

The three oldsters exchanged confused looks. A whirring sweeper bot bumped Zhang Lei's foot. He nudged it away with his toe and headed for the stairs.

Don't be so dramatic, Marta whispered.

"When who comes for you?" Prajapati asked.

"Let them do whatever they want to me," he said. "Don't put yourself in danger. But if you can, keep knocking me out. Please."

Marta sighed. *Honestly.*

You, too. Keep hitting the button. Whatever they do to me, I don't want to know about it.

He climbed the stairs two at a time. If his life was about to be crushed under the boots of a Lunite brawler gang, there was only one thing he wanted to do.

The scarred face of the new moon glared through the high windows of the communal studio. Zhang Lei chose the largest of his prepared canvases and flipped through his viewcatcher compositions. The water buffalo lying in the stream. Jen Dang catching a fish. Ripening rice terraces under golden mist. Jen Dla carrying a pot of sour fish soup, a lock of hair stuck to the sweat of her brow.

The fighting cocks in their cages, separated by the corner of a house, their torn flesh healing only to be sliced open another day.

He flipped the canvas to rest on the long side and projected the composition on its surface. How to make the three-dimensionality of the scene clear in two dimensions—that was the main problem. Each cock knew the other was just out of sight. If they could get free, they would fight to the death.

It's in their nature, he whispered.

What nature? Marta asked. *Oh, I see. Are you going to paint all night?*

I'll paint for the rest of my life.

Okay, ping me if there's a problem.

First, he drafted with a light pencil, adjusting the composition. The corner of the house dividing the canvas into thirds, with one caged brawler directly in front of the viewer and the other around the corner. It was a difficult compositional problem—he had to rub out the draft several times and start again. Then he began a base layer in grays, very lean and thin. What the old masters called *en grisaille.* Solve the painting problems in monochrome before even thinking about color. The texture of the wooden walls of the house, the figures of the birds filling the canvas with belligerence. It took all night.

A few hours before dawn, Han Song brought him a cup of tea.

"That's good," he said, squinting at the canvas. "I've got some pictures of those birds, too." He settled at his workstation and sipped his own tea as he ruffled through his files. "You can use them for reference if you want."

A package hit Zhang Lei's message queue—the only communication he'd received since leaving Luna that didn't relate to his immigration status. The photos were good. Details of the cocks' livid faces and dinosaurian legs, the pinfeathers sprouting from their bald backs, the iridescent sheen of their ruffs.

He added crimson and madder to his palette and used Han Song's photo of the cock's flayed wattle to get that detail exactly right, then moved on to the next problem. He thinned the paint with solvent to make a glaze. No time to wait for fat oils to oxidize, for thick paint layers to cure. In places, the paint was so thin the texture of the canvas showed through. That was fine. He would never be a master painter, but this would be the best painting he could make.

His friend's photos helped. Gradually, color and detail began to bring the painting to life.

"Thank you," Zhang Lei said, hours later. Han Song didn't hear him. Prajapati smiled from across the studio, her hands caked with clay to the elbow.

"Don't skip lunch," she said. "Even painters need to eat."

"And sleep," Paul added.

Sleep. He had no time for it. And Dorgon was in his mattress, behind his door, in his closet. He would join Dorgon soon enough, and next year, when Paizuo's rice crop had turned yellow, they could scream public challenges at each other through a Miao girl.

Until then, there was only the work. Work like he'd never known before. As an athlete, he practiced until instinct overtook his mind. On the ice, he didn't think, he just performed. In the studio, he used his whole body—crouching, stretching, sweeping his arms—continuing the action of his brush far off the canvas like a fighter following a punch past his opponent's jaw. And then small, precise movements—careful, considered, even loving. But his intellect never disengaged. He made choices, second-guessed himself, took leaps of faith.

It was the most exhausting, engrossing work he'd ever done.

The eye of the cock flared on the canvas, trapped in the pointlessness of its drive to fight and fight and die. Zhang Lei hovered his brush over that eye. One more glaze of color, and another, and another, over and over until nobody looking at the painting could misunderstand the meaning of that vicious and brainless stare.

Paul put his arm around Zhang Lei's shoulders.

"Come on down to lunch. The painting is done. If you keep poking, you'll ruin it."

"Ruin yourself, too," said Han Song.

"He's young, he can take it," said Prajapati.

They fed him rice and egg, bitter green tea, and millet cake. No fish soup. No Jen Dla.

"She's giving birth," Prajapati explained. "Went into labor last night. Brave woman."

"We should break out Paul's whiskey again," said Han Song. "Drink a toast to her."

Paul laughed. "Maybe. We have something else to celebrate, too."

They all looked at Zhang Lei. His mouth was crammed with millet cake.

"I don't know. What?" he said though the cake.

"Your button is gone, dear," Prajapati said gently.

He swallowed, pinged his ID. Zhang Lei, Beijing resident. No caveats, no equivocations. And no button.

Marta, he whispered. *Is it done?*

The notice has been sitting in your queue for half an hour. I pinged you when it came through. Looked like you were too busy painting birds to notice.

Are the brawlers gone? he whispered.

They're on their way home. They can't touch you now and they know it. I don't recommend going to Luna anytime soon, but if you did and there was a problem, at least you could fight back.

Zhang Lei excused himself from the table and stumbled out of the guest house. He skirted the cabbage patch and followed the trail to the pavilion, with its perfectly composed view. Up and down the valley, farmers walked the terraces, examining the ripening rice.

How? You said it would be weeks, at least. Maybe never.

I took your painting directly to the tribunal.

That made no sense. His painting was upstairs in the studio, on his easel.

They were impressed, Marta added. *So was I.*

I don't understand.

The wet blood. Smart move. Visceral. The tribunal got the message.

Blood?

On the ice. They brought in a forensic expert to examine and sequence it. That gave me a scare because I had assumed the blood was yours. Didn't even occur to me it might be somebody else's. If it had been, things wouldn't have turned out so well.

My blood?

I guess the tribunal wanted to be convinced you regretted killing Dorgon.

Zhang Lei leaned on the pavilion railing. A fresh breeze ruffled his hair.

I do regret it.

They know that now. I'll keep the painting for you until you get a place of your own. So keep in touch, okay?

I will, he whispered.

On the terrace below, Jen Dang walked along the rice paddy with four of his grandchildren. The farmer waved. Zhang Lei waved back.

The author acknowledges the generous support of the Future Affairs Administration and Danzhai SF Camp.

ABOUT THE AUTHOR

Kelly Robson's short fiction has appeared in *Clarkesworld, Tor.com, Asimov's Science Fiction,* and multiple year's best anthologies. Her book "Gods, Monsters and the Lucky Peach" will be published this March from Tor.com Publishing. In 2017, she was a finalist for the 2017 John W. Campbell Award for Best New Writer. Her novella "Waters of Versailles" won the 2016 Aurora Award and was a finalist for both the Nebula and World Fantasy Awards. She lives in Toronto with her wife, fellow SF writer A.M. Dellamonica.

Waves of Influence

D.A. XIAOLIN SPIRES

"You sent this good for nothing wimp to me?" Her pointed finger inched upwards in the air until it settled on my face. Meixiu pulled back her finger and formed her other hand into a cup, tracing her right finger along the inside of the palm of her left hand. She lowered her voice, whispering to her bot, who stood by her side without moving, "This pimply faced early-twenty-something with small lackluster eyes emanates an aura of unfocused stupidity."

I checked my wrist. Everything she said appeared on her friendgram feed. Scrolling text littered with animated emojis. Then a holo of me formed beside my wrist.

My eyes burned. It was me all right, Chenghui, my likeness standing next to me, the photonic resonance only I could see. But my face was warped even more, the acne magnified, my ears big and droopy made to look like a forlorn dog.

It suddenly felt stuffy in this room, high above ground in one of the tallest skyscrapers in the city. I didn't belong here. Street scum clinging to the whispers of fortune. This is where the rich stood, staring down at the plebes from this sky-high precipice.

"I can hear you, y'know," I said, my voice cool. "And I'm not too stupid to know how to download and read your feed."

"How?"

"I, uh, hacked into your friendgram." I cleared my throat. I hoped she wouldn't expel me right there and then.

Meixiu sighed, waving a hand in the air. "Delete it. The holo. Get rid of it."

The bot dipped its neck, revealing its bald, shiny head.

The glowing message disappeared from my wrist. The holo faded away. I knew it winked away just as it reached the eyes of all in her inner circle.

"Then you know lesson #1. Keep two dreamgrams. One, a truegram, for your following public and another, a friendgram for your close friends."

She swiveled around so I couldn't see her, letting the screen of the back of her leather chair face me. In the screen, she narrowed her eyes. "And pay for the security upgrade, so lurkers can't enter." I saw her arm, slender and practiced, reach out from behind the leather recliner and pull a cup towards her. The same arm put the cup out again, the lipstick on the cup shimmering.

Tiny ticking sounds filled the room, the collective exhale of her twenty-six analog clocks in the room. I had counted while she assessed me stupid.

From behind the recliner, the screen read, "LEAVE." The clocks continued to tick.

Twenty-six stylized clocks told me the same thing. I was almost out of time. Any day now my sister's heart might expire. The doctors said it could be a year, a month, or even a week. I sucked in a breath.

I hoped Meixiu didn't realize I was a fake.

I had stolen a hoverbike, disabled the auto to drive thirty-two miles to get here. My butt was sore, my arms were tired. All for my sister, Yixuan.

I held out the holoticket, projected from my wrist. It was an exact duplicate of the specs that Meixiu had programmed. My name was branded into its digital tapestry as clear as the illumiglass table in front of me. I belonged here, or at least the ticket claimed so.

With this ticket, I was the contest winner and there was no way I was going to let her kick me out. I pushed the glass of water that she had left out towards her, letting it screech along the table. Coasters were not needed with bots at your beck and call to clean and polish.

"The contest rules said that you would teach me," I said to the back of Meixiu's chair, the message of LEAVE on the screen searing into my eyes. "You can't just kick me out the moment I arrive."

From behind the chair I heard a tongue click. The mechanical whir filled the air as she swung back around. Her face was beautiful, near middle-aged with a few wrinkles around the eyes but with that soft touch only a social influencer could have. Her cheeks flawless and blushed. Her eyes sparkled brown and exuded passion. Meixiu enunciated every word with a practiced inflection, an accent that sounded intoxicating. She enchanted all her followers, including Yixuan. Including me. Even if I was only a follower for the last few weeks and not the years my account claimed. "I asked for only serious apprentices to enter the contest."

"But, I am a serious apprentice—"

She gave me an up and down, the quick jerk of her head for a second disturbed her makeup, the augmented tech hiccup before it settled back layered onto her face.

"You come in here without any cosmetic enhancements and tell me you're serious? You're going to show that face to the public?" Her lips turned down.

I threw my arms up. "But social influencers are supposed to be authentic!" I touched my cheeks, feeling the rough texture of craters. Yixuan and I both shared the fate of bad complexion.

"Then, that's lesson #2. You're supposed to exude authenticity. Not wipe your programs of any blemish-removers. I'd be surprised if anyone wanted your holo floating around their rooms. If you can't understand that basic point, then there's no way to teach you." She shut her eyes. The quick flutter caused the augmented eyeshadow to hover for a few zeptoseconds. It was barely visible, but my illegal perception enhancements made this moment of disjointed layering all too clear.

The clocks ticked. It was unnerving, all those analog needles making noises. These social influencers always lead the latest trends in purchases. I wonder how many women my age and younger were sporting analog clocks on their wrists because of her. I counted a few seconds and watched again, waiting for her to blink.

There, there it was. The layering dissonance.

"You missed an upgrade," I said.

"What?" She rubbed her temples.

"Your eyelids."

"Jacoby, mirror."

The blank screen on the bot's face turned reflective. Its head moved down its chest, guided along by the crane neck until it was at Meixiu's eyes. Her pupils contracted as the light from the bot hit her face. She fluttered her eyelashes, a dainty movement of grace that made even my heart pound. The eyeshadow lapse didn't really take away from her beauty.

"You're right. I'll recalibrate. Good thing I didn't send out any holoselfies in the last ten minutes."

She gave me a look. "Come closer, you. Chengli or whatever."

"Name's Chenghui."

"Alright, Chenghui." She beckoned.

I stepped up, head high, still waving, projecting my ticket. This projection was set to viewable to public, meaning it emitted photonic resonance that anyone in my physical vicinity could see.

"Turn that off," she said. "I already know you've won."

I heaved a sigh of relief. She didn't notice my hack.

"Jacoby, move the light to capture her profile."

She picked up a brush from the holder on her table. The bristles were not as wispy as they looked and landed on my cheeks hard. I could almost feel the wisps of digital paint being applied on. I thought of Yixuan. What she would do to feel the touch of Meixiu's artistry.

"Ah, that's better. This'll work for now. Now, take this holoselfie and put it up. Call it the 'before' and tag it with #InfluencerApprenticeContest. You're the winner and you better believe that I'll make you one. All your followers will see my work."

"I only have ten."

"Ten? What have you been doing on there all this time? Well, that'll have to change. Put this holo up and send me your profile."

I raised my wrist. A pane of light moved from the top of my head down to the bottom. I added Meixiu to my list of "bosombuddies."

"On second thought, add some of these wardrobe accessories before you post your holo."

A ping indicated I received a gift of two necklaces and a dress. Some facial adjustments also arrived my way.

"That's a Locklie Dree dress. And two Connie Wu Spring series from twenty years ago. We're gonna bring it back."

A buzz indicated the holo was done rendering. I projected my holo out, with the setting so that it was viewable to anyone in the room.

The bottom lobes of my ears didn't droop unevenly and my eyes looked alert and bright. The A-line dress flattered my hips, as the holo swayed, sashaying in place.

"It's . . . alright. Needs work, but this is the 'before' after all. The blue at least brings out some color in your otherwise lifeless eyes."

"Thanks," I said. Inside I felt a giddiness rising up from my chest. Step one was complete. Meixiu had linked directly to my system.

"Should I upload it now?"

"Yes, post it."

I made a few swipes on my wrist. I blushed as this holoselfie would suddenly appear beside the ten girls, my followers across the globe. I could imagine this version of me appearing next to them in their rooms or alongside them as they went shopping at the fashion museums, as they marked items down behind glass for reproduction in their replibox. Right now, all these copies of me were popping up, virtual but admired. *The contest winner.* I'd probably only be there for the ten seconds before they scrolled to something else, but already I felt like I was moving in the right direction.

I couldn't help it. Excitement filled my chest. I was gloating.

"On my way to influencing," I said, smiling to myself. I looked at Meixiu, "Thanks to you, my social queen." I was being facetious, but she didn't notice.

"Just call me, Meixiu." She put her arms behind her head and leaned back. "The influencer who makes influencers," she said. "Not bad huh? It was really Jacoby's idea. Crunched all the numbers—a marketing move no one has tried before. It might just work." She pulled up a mannequin wearing a silk vest.

"Now, if you'll excuse me. I have work to do. Negotiating my next contract with one of the ads."

"Anything I can do?" I wrapped my hands around each other in front of my body.

She shook her head.

"I can't help you with influencing any more today. It tires me. Besides I have this ad contract and other stuff to do. I have a pile of offerings to sort at the replibox. All these fans and companies sending me stuff. I have to see what I can sell and what I'll need to repurpose."

I thought fast. I was losing her. I had to work my way in, get access quick. Yixuan was fading, her heart giving way. "I can do that. I'll do the sorting. Inventory. I'm good at it."

Meixiu gave me a quizzical look. Her lips pursed together in a way I remembered from her holoselfie two days ago. She was wearing a mandarin collar dress then. Stately but elegant.

"Fine. Jacoby will help you."

I heaved a sigh. I was in.

I'm here, I thought. *Not to emulate you, but to be you.*

There were a million ways to make money and I could probably try my hand at hacking one of the cryptocurrencies, one of the smaller ones with less security. It would be more direct, faster, though probably subject to closer scrutiny. I could gain control of accounts and blackmail. I could try to steal proprietary information and sell it in an act of industrial espionage. I wouldn't be the best, but I could train myself. I was sly and proficient.

But, it wasn't about the money. I was content with being poor, for the most part. We've been poor all our lives.

This was for Yixuan. She wanted this. All those days she sat around, staring at Meixiu's holo, mumbling, "Look at her. Her silken hair. Her cool, sexy style." Showering her with praise. Even as Yixuan's heart started to give way, her eyes lit up when a Meixiu truegram update came in. But, it wasn't enough. There was a hunger in her eyes, a look of discontent. If I could just be Meixiu, then she'd hold on. She needed an influencer that could shower her with the attention she deserved. As Meixiu, I would constantly be sending her virtual messages, personally crafted, a holo just for her by her side. She'd look up to me, hang onto me as that thread of hope.

I stared at a limb that I held in my hand. It looked real but felt light as a feather. The fingers were long, like a piano player's, the nails were painted in metallic blue, the color of Meixiu's eyes. Why would anyone recreate their arms and fingers and send it over to Meixiu? It was gross. Luckily, it was only a mylofoam reproduction. Organic reproduction was only allowed for certain specifications in the replibox. Only items in the preapproved list: food, medicine, clothing, and some others. And luckily Meixiu had the upgrades in, so no true-to-life reproductions of heads or organs could be sent her way.

I shook my head and tossed the fake limb into the "reprocess" pile. It would cost Meixiu more creds to dissolve the item rather than just selling it off whole in the replibox. There was the reprocessing fee. But, I doubt anyone would want this thing. The "reprocess" pile was growing. *Who would do this? Send this here?*

Fans, I thought, reaching for a gold watch. *Fans send a lot of junk.* I scratched the surface with a fingernail. The gold flaked off.

Fans like my sister.

I grabbed the pile for reprocessing, holding it in my arms, which Jacoby scanned to double check. He sent the details to Meixiu whose consent I received. *Burn them.*

I put a few pieces—fake limbs, painted portraits, jars of unidentified fluids—into the replibox and set it for reprocessing. Dissolve. A flash of warmth filled the air as they were "burned" into potential particulates and drained cred from the owner's account. These particulates siphoned into the chamber behind the box where they held in stasis until an order came in for production. Usually people sent items that already had fixed forms. It was way cheaper to pass on things as-is than to embed a reform command. I remember one of my mechoteachers said it was about the quantum costs of transformation, but reconstructional physics was never one of my best subjects.

Once the burn was through and the fan donations and promotional junk were nothing but digital debris, awaiting costly reformation, I went back to fetch more junk. Air-filled balloons (but not with highly coveted helium, but just regular mCO2), fake ivory chopsticks, faux jade canteens: Was anything real anymore? I stacked them again in the replibox, balancing them like a game.

I remembered the game I used to play with Yixuan, stacking up the plastobins we used as kitchenware in our house. Here they use illumiglass, and plastobins never had the same shine. We would stack them into "buildings" after dinner, adding chopsticks as antennae. Then we'd smack them, watching them fall. Their translucent durable sides would collide and tumble onto the ground, the chopsticks clattering onto the mylopropylene tiles. Mom would then force us to wipe up the mess, saying that if we messed up those containers, we had no cred to reform more. She would look so serious before breaking into a smile. Mom whose smile I missed so much, before it faded away, like her physical strength in her last days.

I thought about her frail arms, her weak legs. They said the sickness was genetic, but the gene bypassed me.

I balanced the chopsticks in the faux jade canteens. The chopsticks shone with artificial gleam.

I pressed the burn and felt a wave of heat as a zigzag pattern burned in my retinas for a moment before I blinked them away.

Those were the days before Yixuan got sick, before she could hardly lift a chopstick, let alone jab a punch at plastobin towers. Since then, she'd been sitting in bed at the hospice, upsticking holoselfies of social celebs, talking in exaggerated form. Meixiu was her favorite, a shimmering figure of grace appearing at her bed at least three times a day. Yixuan kept refreshing Meixiu's truegram feed. Her fingers twitched, always wanting more.

I kicked the pile before me. A stitched towel and a rattling can flew up into the air and landed back down. The stitched towel covered up the face of a green-eyed polyporcelain doll. The can rolled away.

Junk. All this junk. I bet some of these things might be ours. We had no cred to speak of to reform things, but Yixuan could have zapped something straight over to Meixiu without the transformation fee.

I walked back to the pile, took a glance at the unsorted goods. Nothing that looked familiar. Good.

Just piles of merch and junk. The fortunes amassed by highly-followed social influencers.

Their living, their earnings—refuse of the late twenty-first century.

The next day, Meixiu slinked in wearing a sequined Gustav Chen dress.

"The fashion museums are awfully crowded. I couldn't even lock onto the Ying Rodriguez scarf before it dissipated in favor of the next line."

"Sounds pretty awful," I said. I looked at her mascaraed lashes. I wondered if that was the right response.

Meixiu waved a hand. She made some motions with her wrist and her holoselfie from earlier today appeared, her red sequins glinting in the fashion museum lights, her slender form shifting into poses, foregrounding the illumiglass cases that held brand name purses and jewelry. Her holoselfie gave a flirtatious kiss.

I pretended to catch the kiss. Meixiu approved, chuckling. I smiled.

"I don't understand why you even go there. Why don't you just fabricate the background like most holo-posters?"

"Then it wouldn't be authentic," she said. "Besides, I need to get out sometimes. It's good for followers to spot me and take surreptitious holophotos of me and my merch. My sponsoring corporations love that."

She studied her own holoform for a few more moments before swiping it away. Another celeb filled her view, blonde hair, hefty shoulders, and a robust chest, wearing a black leather suit.

"Not bad. Take notes," she said to Jacoby. His screen reflected the swagger of this Lisa W. Zhao and he tried copying the moves, making us both laugh.

I had to admit it. Meixiu may be performed and artful, but she had the strange humor of a celeb who knew she was passing. Like a moth flying into the light, she continued to flaunt her feminine mystique even as she was becoming passé.

In the last few days, it was clear to me that her influence was dying. That was why she was trying harder to make appearances, to put herself on the scene. But it didn't matter, she could be blowing up like the next Jachoo or becoming a social cadaver like Sayne Wang. All that mattered was Yixuan was into her. It was all for her. Yixuan was fiercely loyal and would stay following her, probably looking up to her like the way I hoped she looked up to me.

Meixiu kept scrolling across her home feeds, keeping up with what the other influencers were posting. She had to strike a delicate balance, taking a stance of a particular lifestyle and brand, displaying a brazen uniqueness while not deviating too far from the norm. At least that's what she admitted, as another one of her lessons.

Through my last few days of tinkering around in her tech, I found that she used the Mikst 24-K layering system. I read up on all the proprietary specs I could get my hands on. It meant all I needed was to steal the imprint of a particular memory to unlock her account.

I would need that specific memory, along with her physical trace, a ghosting of her vitals, then I could take her identity and biosear it to my own. From there, I could gain access to her replibox and transfer it to our encrypted one—the one I shared with Yixuan, which would at least supply us with some merch to pay off the hospital debts. It was more so that Yixuan could get some of that scrap she coveted: bracelets and beaded broaches and whatever.

I just wanted to see her face light up, happy. I wanted to be the hero in her heart, to wipe away the digital imprints of all those other fakes that took up her existence. If I could become Meixiu, even momentarily, then she would look up to me. And it wouldn't work just to layer on a costume. As a huge social consumer, even savvier than me, Yixuan would sniff out the difference right away. I would have to graft Meixiu's existence onto my own.

And I needed to find that memory.

Over the course of the week, Meixiu visited the museums, then spent time prancing around landmarks, trying to create a romantic concept for her brand. She told me all about it. As her apprentice, I followed her sometimes, taking my own holos against bridges over canals, grand pagodas, and marble plazas. I had my own following of about a few hundred now.

"Not bad," she said. "You have to work on your expressions. Even the maneuver layering won't fix up your vacant eyes."

Meixiu had me sorting through her donations, even letting me take a few keepers of my own. Necklaces and belts, teeth cleaning powders and lip brighteners. I had to accept them to make myself seem like I was really interested.

I experimented with all kinds of smiles and winks, practiced an exercise she called cheekbone lifts. She gave me a massager to level out what she called the uneven surfaces of my skin. She also gifted me an "Allure Cure" and we sat together, rolling these tiny balls over our pores, pulling at what she called the "magnetic presence of beauty," letting this essence draw through our skin.

Every day we talked, but I could not get her to speak about her past. Not a peep about her life outside brands and glamorous concepts. She just spoke about her marketing philosophies and her approaches to stardom. Sometimes she joked around about Jacoby and other bots of the past, but nothing that triggered any memory curls in the security system.

Scrolling through her feeds offered no help. The few glimpses of life outside commercialism and grandeur—beach strolls, music concerts, feeding birds in parks—gave me little to work with. How could someone project such authenticity with such a shallow set of coordinates? The more I stayed with her, the more confounded I became. It seemed so obvious. There was no substance here, but people were drawn to her as real. As alive, charismatic, and full of verve and life.

Rituals became automatic to me. Daily habits: checking my reflection in Jacoby's converted mirror, applying upscale digital foundations set at various levels of opacity and rubbing in the maquillage. The constant changes of outfits and the periodic body sweeps to realign wardrobe measurements. The pulling and pinching of skin that was supposed to brighten my chromatic schema for better layering. Strolling through set-like landscapes to make my intrigue more pronounced.

If Meixiu was stunning, graceful, and passionate, then I was made to be cool, dainty and carefree. She said my lifeless eyes were the biggest hurdle. She couldn't make me alluring if I wasn't expressive naturally. I told her I thought everything could be layered on, like glazing on pottery. But, she said I was as plain as an old-fashioned clay pot, and the layering could only disguise, not revolutionize.

But, I did feel a metamorphosis blooming within me—and I wasn't sure if that was why I kept my holos on all the time, drawn to my own holoselfies like they were phantoms of my existence propping me up.

In those weeks, I visited Yixuan less and less, until one day an alert popped up. It was an alert I set up during the first few days of Meixiu's tutelage.

I tracked the many devious turns through the digital jungle that led me to the ID. The alert didn't lie. It was Yixuan. She was my follower.

I didn't think she realized that it was me. I had since deleted my original "befores" that I posted months before, making sure to leave no trace of that unsightly past in my truefeed portfolio.

I held my posture high, my chin up. My face was without blemishes and constantly covered with digital layering. We bought new layering tech so that we could enhance the grid, sharpen the twinkle of my perfectly aligned teeth and balance the smudge of the rouge so its evenness could ride over my cheekbones with the gliding smoothness of a crane in flight. The tailcoats of my signature asymmetric miniskirts fluttered behind me, shouting *cute* and *delightful*, as I trailed next to Meixiu. We often had posted holos together. Her hand clasped in mine, her smile as wide as my own. Her lips upturned in mystique, mine with a playful gap, exposing tongue and teeth, inviting *fun* and *adventure*.

It wasn't that I forgot about Yixuan. It was all for her after all.

It was just that I got caught up on the brand metrics, the digital outfitting algorithms, the crunching of follower numbers. I got swept away in the brands that covered me, buffered me from the petty thing I was inside with layers and layers, building up a story that I couldn't keep up with.

And one day, in Meixiu's replicator, I got an arm. An arm that looked just like Yixuan's. Half-moon nails in glitter and glow, just like she liked it.

It was mylofoam, of course. Nothing else could get through. But something creeped me out about it. It was as fake as the glimmering lipstick that stuck to the fabric as I gave it a kiss.

Didn't know why I did it. Or maybe I did.

It reminded me of home, or some phantasmic rendering of it.

It must have been a year since I visited Yixuan.

It wasn't that I didn't want to go. It was just that I couldn't be seen in the hospice. People would think I was dying. My ratings would fall, my followers would leave. Besides it's not like she needed me, she just needed the ideal projection of grace—a holo to turn to.

I had left Yixuan holomessages then, stripped of my layerings and often curt. This layerless being, it no longer felt like me. Conversely, they felt like some spectacle of me, a perversion, like I had removed my skin and my entrails were showing.

How much do we gain and shed until we are our real selves? What is the real underneath the real? Are they overlays or removals? I couldn't tell but it didn't really matter.

I tried to convince Meixiu to come with me, but she wouldn't go near that part of town. She didn't understand my deviant fascination with the morbid.

"Is this some new trend?" she asked. "I don't think it's going to work. The macabre went out decades ago and never came back. There are a few loners out there that go for it, but it'll definitely kill your cute brand. And my mystique can't handle a blow like that. You know I'm starting to show my age."

"Philanthropy," I said. "Goodwill sells." But, she knew as much as I did that it was a pathetic plea. She was right, of course. The stench of death was a brand-killer. Maybe it was better this way. I didn't want her to suspect my past, even if I wanted some support to hang onto.

None of that conversation was caught in the digital entries of manicured holoselfies of our feeds. Those were the conversations uttered in lapses, swept under, not fit for viral consumption.

I prepped for my trip. It felt like a journey to the land of unknown. Not sweeping landscapes and imposing statues polished to lustrous perfection, but a hospice. I tried on a new layering that fit my cute self, but also eclipsed some of my recognizable features. It dampened the effect of my bold, ruddy cheeks, dimmed the glitter of my teeth. Still, I stood out in the dreary town, in the waiting room, hanging around the morbid near-dead.

Luckily the staff knew I could never stay in a room like that so long. They told me someone would be out soon to usher me into her room.

I fretted. I knew she was comfortable. I made Jacoby make sure of that. Jacoby never knew where all the stuff was going. Meixiu didn't have the hacking instinct in her bones to program him to follow, not even a bit. The directions were rerouted and re-encrypted in so many ways, an intricate labyrinth that misled at every turn.

But, I wrote the instructions carefully. Eventually these things would get to the hospice. Eventually, they would get to her. She would have some merch and clean sheets. Nurses hired to look after her.

They called me in. They walked in regulation sneakers, I sashayed in silver Viggo Lee's. They left as soon as they showed me the room. There were many rooms, many patients. They were busy.

I placed my hand on the door. It was faded, old. I pushed it open.

When she saw me, it was like she saw a god.

I walked in, stood by the seat that was planted next to her. By that point, I had surpassed Meixiu in follower numbers. Crowned "Influencer Maximus" in one of the major Social Influencer awards. We often worked together, so Meixiu didn't mind my achievements, but I remembered the day it happened. The day I superseded her. Meixiu covered up bleary, swollen eyes with extra rendering around the upper half of her face. I could tell. My perceptions were always better than hers. We never talked about it.

I saw the pile of merch at the foot of the hospital bed. The stuff I rerouted to her. I looked at the girl in the bed before me, almost a woman now. Her eyes wide, worshipping.

Yixuan.

Something in my heart jumped a little. But, not quite enough.

All I could see was something so plain and so small. Insignificant. A number on my extended followers' list. Someone who loved me for who I truly was. Magnificent, stellar, cool, and sexy.

I convinced myself I didn't care. I stared at her dull lips and pallor, so obvious through her one digital layer of frecklesalve. Her nervous eyes flickered, full of enthusiasm and naïveté, even in her bedridden state. Her skin was pasty, a sallow yellow. I knew she was sick. There was a part of me that felt disgusted, a part sickened by her and myself. A part that knew I should care, felt that I did, but couldn't be bothered to be informed to do anything otherwise. I just stood there.

I smiled, dropping my lower lip to show off my splendid teeth and said one of my signature phrases.

"Adventures come from within. Let's share them together."

Something weighty and loaded fell on me then. It felt like something broke through the sky and landed on my head. It wasn't anything real. Maybe a digital hiccup, a layering issue that messed with my perceptions, besmirched my immaculate algorithm of cover-up.

I felt exposed then, as something heavy plunged into my heart.

I touched her hand, felt warmth. I hooked my fingers in hers and some pressure wiggled within. It seemed like an improbable feeling, a jolt that ran through my arms, a memory that surged from long ago.

When I was little I carried you in my arms.

We went swimming, the ocean washing away all the sand from our skin, from playing sandcastles earlier, a game needing no materials but plastobins. Mom was chatting with a fellow beachgoer. You and I, we dove in. Icy cold, enlivening. It was clear water and we splashed, nonchalant, carefree. The waves lapped, gentle rises and falls on the surface. But, as you were yapping away, describing the sandcastle you planned to make upon our return to land, the waves rose suddenly and one tore through, knocking us out of our leisurely strokes. I desperately looked for you, saw an imprint from below the surface, warped and colorful, a billowing sheet of clothing and skin, and reached in.

I pulled you up and brought you to shore, carried you in my arms, dripping, sopping, as Mom stood there agape and later crying. You were all right, and you went off to build your castle . . .

But the memory stuck with me.

I let go of that hand, let it fall. I left all that merch and that sick figure on the bed.

I rushed out of that hospice, my miniskirt coattails flying, feeling exposed, followed, a sticky cloying heaviness that gained on me, making my typically light footsteps of the Viggo Lee's fall in a strangely heavy tread.

That memory came to me every so often. Water all around us, washing away sand, the dirt between our fingers. The fresh saltwater washing away everything, drawing me to you. Holding you safe.

It was the memory that someone used to hack my system, years later, when I no longer uploaded holos with Meixiu.

I unleashed all my hacking prowess, had creepers that followed all the routes, all the entangled courses, but to no avail.

I never knew who it was.

All I did was rock back and forth, sitting in my merch, wondering what I should burn and what to keep. I remembered holding a mylofoam limb, so ghastly and all kitsch, yearning for my royal social crown, the ticks and tocks of life I could never go back and retrieve.

I gave the limb a kiss and watched my glimmering coral lipstick fade from its smooth, cold surface. The ticks and tocks remained the same, never fading, never faster, never slower, the same pitch, perfectly paced, persistent.

ABOUT THE AUTHOR

D.A. Xiaolin Spires steps into portals and reappears in sites such as Hawai'i, NY, various parts of Asia and elsewhere, with her keyboard appendage attached. Her work appears or is forthcoming in publications such as *Clarkesworld, Analog, Nature, Terraform, Grievous Angel, Fireside, Galaxy's Edge, StarShip-Sofa, Andromeda Spaceways* (Year's Best Issue), *Diabolical Plots, Factor Four, Pantheon, Outlook Springs, ROBOT DINOSAURS, Mithila Review, LONTAR, Reckoning, Issues in Earth Science, Liminality, Star*Line, Polu Texni, Argot, Eye to the Telescope, Liquid Imagination, Gathering Storm Magazine, Little Blue Marble, Story Seed Vault,* and anthologies of the strange and beautiful: *Ride the Star Wind, Sharp and Sugar Tooth, Future Visions, Deep Signal, Battling in All Her Finery,* and *Broad Knowledge.*

She can be found on Twitter: @spireswriter.

Dandelion

ELLY BANGS

It was a century ago today that you found the spark of life in this freeze-dried valley of death. The ghost of you in that moment is here with me now, Geiger counter in hand, sifting in holy awe through the wind-polished stones—to which your daughter would make her own heartbroken pilgrimage thirty years later—to which I've finally come in my turn. When I breathe in, I feel how this same frigid wind scalded your lungs as you climbed, shielding your eyes against the midnight sun. On the other side of the world, your family huddled in the glow of a cathode ray tube and wondered if that sun would ever rise on them again.

My mother would have been five years old then, in October 1961. That became her earliest memory: her father cursing you for being off in some God-forsaken Antarctic valley on the eve of doomsday; she only wishing you'd taken her with you, out of range of Cuban missiles—but in the fullness of time you redeemed yourself, because that was the day you brought back what would become an heirloom, passed across the whole breadth of the sky by way of three generations of this family, shaping all of our lives along the way.

The Agency called it "Sputnik-X," but you knew better—already intuiting, years before you dared to speak it, the truth of what you found half-buried in this desiccated scree. You called it Dandelion.

To you it was the key to a universe of ambition. To my mother it was a warning and a reality check. To me it's the point at which the forces of hope and despair meet and become something greater, and that's why yours is the memory I've come here to commune with: because you died, grandmother, believing that your life's work had been for nothing.

Since then it's changed everything.

• • •

The object weighs approximately six tons. It is radioactive. Its metal is mottled with corrosion, filed down by gritty wind and slow tides of heating and cooling through year-long polar days, but it remains at first glance a machine made to fall from space: One end is capped with a blasted heat shield, the other with fasteners for a long-lost parachute; between them two cylinders sit stacked in a nest of tubes and fins. One contains a pile of black fissile slag. The other is empty.

I've only seen Dandelion once in person. After your daughter gave them Plateau Theory, the Agency bitterly entombed it in a New Mexico salt mine with no intention of ever raising it again—but despite the Agency's basic hatred of me after what I did, my connections at NASA were enough to grant me one visit.

I'd spent years imagining that moment. I thought when I touched that metal I'd be able to feel the vastness of space it crossed to reach us, the centuries of vacuum and cosmic rays, but for a moment I could feel much more: It was as if I could sense its makers touching back from the other side, their hands (by any other name) to mine, and I knew they were as much a part of my heritage as you are.

It took me years after your death to feel as if I knew you. Not just the version of you I spent Sundays with—who lashed out at her caretakers, disowned her daughter, and died hating the world for its inertia—but your original form. I read all of your journals and talked to anyone left to testify. Some called you cold and aloof, not getting that you built your life around a fierce and unwavering love. That it wasn't for the people around you doesn't lessen its reality. You cared about them, but it was the possible you were in love with—and if ever that abstract concept loved any person back, you were her.

You married because you hadn't yet found a language with which to question the necessity; because when you told him you needed to put your career first, he was naïve enough about himself to promise he would respect that. By the time my mother was born he was living in the perceived shadow of men whose wives fed and cleaned up after them, and you'd begun to suspect there was something other women got out of having families, a sense of belonging that you'd never felt and probably never would.

Your house was just a house. It was in the concrete-slab laboratories of the Advanced Projects Research Agency that you found your home. Mathematics was your love language and the arc of orbital space was the set of arms you embraced with every satellite you helped launch from Vandenburg.

You were one of the Agency's brightest minds—and the higher you rose, the harder it worked to throw you out.

You wouldn't have been their first choice for the job if they'd had any idea what the job was. You recognized the taunt when you saw it: Somewhere along the line you'd intimidated your male colleagues, so they were sending you to the bottom of the world to chase a vague report of radioactive space debris. One of those upstairs men with a haircut sharp as a helipad was putting his wingtips up and reasoning that a wife and a mother would never agree to weeks of hard travel away from family—that her family wouldn't let her. He didn't expect you to call his bluff, and in doing so break the game.

"You said it was just sitting out there," their voices rang through the cargo bay. "Left sitting out for a *month* before you got there. Not even a tarp over it."

"Two months," you corrected, drowsily, as twenty men in suits (some in hazmat, others in single-breasted black linen) rushed into the C-130 that had delivered you and Dandelion to them over forty hours of flight. "But it was so remote that—"

"This is a disaster."

"Why the hell didn't anyone get to it sooner?"

You could've explained the challenges of airlifting a six-ton object out of the Dry Valleys during Antarctic Winter, but you knew they were really asking for someone to blame. For you being the one to find it.

"The question is how did the Soviets get this thing into space without us knowing."

"How did they get it into space *at all?* What rocket can throw a six-ton payload?"

"But what if it's not—?" you started, but the flattop men were already forgetting you were there.

"No," one interrupted. "The real question is *what* the hell is it."

"Spy satellite."

"Anti-satellite weapon."

"Gentlemen. Given its mass, its radioactivity, and where it was found, there can be no doubt that we are looking at a nearly successful prototype of a Fractional Orbital Bombardment System."

A funereal silence fell as your colleagues concluded that their Russian counterparts were twenty years ahead of them in missile technology. The irony would haunt you for the rest of your life: that Dandelion had chosen one of the unluckiest moments in history to be discovered, right when it risked setting in motion the death of the planet it would have brought to life.

You wanted to grab those men by the lapels and shake them. *Wait*, you shouted, inwardly. *Just wait.*

From 1961 to 1964, the top-secret project to analyze and reverse-engineer "Sputnik X" waded through a quicksand of bad assumptions. By the design standards of the time it was a monstrosity, sheathed in two-inch-thick plates of beryllium alloy, bolted to a heat shield twice as thick as Earth's atmosphere required. There were clues that Dandelion had come from much farther away than Kazakhstan, but no one dared to follow a line of inquiry that veered so sharply away from the Project's rigidly-defined goals. The radioactive slag in the upper cylinder was assumed to be the remains of an experimental bomb core that had fizzled or self-destructed upon loss of contact with its Russian operators. It was the enigma of the empty lower cylinder that haunted everyone's nightmares.

You weren't alone in wondering if that black slag might be the remains not of a weapon but a power source: a long-expired radioisotope thermoelectric generator. You weren't the only one to count the elements and trace their half-lives, following the decay chains backward through time to reconstruct their pure original form. A dozen of your colleagues did the same math, rubbed their eyes, and moved on to avenues of research less likely to get them fired.

You weren't the only one to see the data. You were just the only one willing to believe Dandelion when it told you it was 1.7 million years old.

It wasn't easy to convince the McMurdo Station people, and moreover my wife, to drop a 71-year-old woman off in Victoria Valley and leave her alone for a while, but it had to be done. I knew I could only make this pilgrimage by myself.

On the flight in, we passed a glacier that looks like it's spewing blood. It's more spectacular today than when you saw it, now that all the glaciers are rapidly melting. The red stuff percolates up through a thousand feet of ice, from a lake of iron-rich brine. A whole ecosystem of extremophile bacteria lives down there in the pitch-black, sealed airtight for a very long time.

Around 1.7 million years, in fact.

It's probably a coincidence: We can't prove these are the same germs that rode Dandelion across space. Still, they're perfect for the job—simple, hardy, cold-loving—and in long hours spent watching them grow in vats, I've whispered under my breath the same two-word prayer you taught me as a child:

What if?

It's the question I hear the whole world asking these days. The poles are still melting. The oceans are still gaining plastic and losing oxygen. We're all wading through the rising tide of our worst fears—but I believe they temper a hope that's more than worthy even of your Golden Age optimism. The nations of Earth are putting away their weapons and joining the work in orbit, and what we're building up there is a symbol of all we hope to fix below. Through Dandelion we're becoming supplicants of the possible. We've found a purpose to work toward—and by God, we're finally working together.

One day you were the Agency's black sheep, the next you were its champion. Every new data point bolstered your theory of Dandelion's ancient extraterrestrial origin. Under your leadership the miasma of paranoid despair that had dogged the Project since its inception gave way to a renaissance of hope and imagination, its subject transformed from an inscrutable Soviet superweapon into the tantalizing promise of a million-year technological leap.

By 1965 you hadn't just figured out Dandelion's age: you'd intuited its purpose. Outside your concrete slab walls, Sagan and Shklovskii were speaking publicly to a theory you'd been incubating for years: that the first life on Earth had been delivered here deliberately.

You'd found the delivery system. You knew the answers to questions human beings had lived and died to ask since the dawn of recorded time: You knew where we'd come from. You knew we weren't alone. Above all you, were sure you knew what we'd become.

We will live on the moon, you wrote, your handwriting skewed by exuberance. *We will live on Mars and the moons of Jupiter, and on distant planets orbiting distant stars in distant galaxies. We'll build cities in space and a glittering network of wormhole highways, stretching from one end of the sky to the other, lined with ring worlds and Dyson spheres and wonders we cannot yet fathom. We have our proof that all this and infinitely more is possible. I've held it in my own hands.*

"So the second cylinder, the empty one, carried . . . primordial ooze?" a younger scientist once asked you.

"Single-celled organisms," you said, pacing and gesticulating wildly. "Ones suited to extreme environments. Capable of spreading and evolving over eons into an entire planetary biosphere."

"But life on Earth is much older than Dandelion," she said.

"Dandelion itself isn't the origin of life here, but it's evidence of that origin, proof that directed panspermia is happening. Another seed from the same tree, billions of years later. Just think of it! Countless probes must have reached Earth from one end of geologic history to the other. All the rest are weathered to dust, subducted, lost to the ocean floor—"

"But Dandelion just happened to land in the coldest, driest place on Earth," she said, and your heart melted at the epiphany in her voice, her face, her whole body as she put it together.

"If you were trying to seed planets with life you'd *want* thousands of probes, wouldn't you?" she said. "You'd plant as many seeds as possible, knowing some won't germinate."

You started to tell her your theories about the whole seed-head of which Dandelion had been a part, the methods of hyperlight propulsion that might have carried it between galaxies, but your voice caught. Your pulse quickened. The beach stretched away in either direction, smoke plumes looming peacefully from the oil rigs just off shore. There were no spooks in sight, but you couldn't be sure.

"You can't tell anyone about this," you whispered. "Remember that. Not *anyone.*"

"I know, mom!" my mother protested.

I believe the love you had for her in those years was the purest you ever shared with another person. To be united in the elemental joy of discovery was the only kind of kinship you'd ever really wanted. You could open up to her in ways that you couldn't to the detail-obsessed, goal-oriented scientists under your direction. What Margaret initially lacked in formal education she made up for with unbridled awe, and the threat of being fired if not imprisoned for leaking highly classified information to your own daughter only strengthened the bond.

You had a seemingly magical way of encouraging her in her studies without making her feel bad when she struggled. You believed her success was inevitable, and convinced her of the same. She was driven to see Dandelion for herself, and you told her exactly how she'd need to steer the course of her young life to make it happen—until finally the day came in 1988 when you welcomed her through the gates. It might have been the proudest moment of your life.

Thirty years on, she would tell me it was the one she most wished she could take back.

Radioactive decay elevated you to leadership of the Project, but the Project had its own decay process. For three decades your team had searched every micron of Dandelion's shell for nanoscale circuitry, magnetic signatures, golden-record-style grooves that might encode data: Something you could make into free energy or antigravity or faster-than-light propulsion. By 1988 you'd compiled tens of thousands of pages of theory and speculation, but you had nothing tangible to show for it. Some of your staff quit; others stayed on and let the years of stagnation sand their minds smooth.

You were sure Margaret was the new blood the Project needed. You loomed over her, waiting to witness a spark of epiphany. When she asked to make her own expedition to the crash site to search for more debris, you rushed to authorize it, never guessing the depth of her restlessness.

She was here on the same dry ground I'm hiking now. When every lidar and spectroscopic and visual survey came back empty, she sifted through these rocks by hand. Her apparition is just as present in this place as yours, staggering along under the weight of all her prayers that she would find something here to prove herself wrong.

Anything but to explain to you why there were no more breakthroughs left to have.

In February 1990, Voyager 1 took one last look back on its way to interstellar space, transmitting a mosaic of the Solar System in which the Earth appears as a lonely pale blue dot. Over the next thirty years the probe's RTGs (not unlike Dandelion's) would decay until they could no longer generate enough power to communicate with Earth—and while it was beaming back its final pixels, Margaret was making her last attempt to communicate with you, and feeling just as distant and as cold.

"You've been trapped in your precepts," she told you. "You taught me that a good scientist has to see past her assumptions when they don't align with the facts, no matter what. She has to—"

"What assumptions?" you protested. "The idea of progress? The idea of a better future? The idea of a future at all?"

"You're being hyperbolic."

"Am I?" You paced the floor, scraping your shoes against the Cold War tiled floor.

"You're director," she said, evenly. "You have the authority to block me from submitting this report. Are you going to do that?"

To her it was a practical question, but you heard it as a dare: to prove you were any better than your own flattopped predecessors. Suppressing her report would be tantamount to surrender: She had to take it back of her own free will.

You settled on: "Not until I know you understand what's at stake."

She took a deep breath and said "I'm not saying we've seen the end of *all* technological advance. Every technology will have its own plateau. Some lie farther ahead than others. I'm talking about space travel specifically."

"But without that—" You trailed off, afraid to finish saying: *What's the point of anything? What's the point of humanity?*

She continued: "You've only ever studied Dandelion from the assumption that technological progress accelerates forever. Like Moore's Law. And it makes sense that would feel plausible—"

You snorted derisively at the word *feel.*

"—earlier in this century. Cars, airplanes, rockets, nuclear power, digital computers—they all emerged within a single lifetime. Manned interstellar flight and galactic empire-building *seem* like logical next steps, but everything we know about Dandelion contradicts that."

"What contradicts that?" you said. Still pacing. "What exactly do you think contradicts it?"

"You've read my report. Come on, mom."

"*Ma'am,*" you corrected—and you looked at each other, both knowing you'd passed the point of no return and were headed out into the real dark.

Now you were the one daring her. She stiffened up and said "We know all of Dandelion's metals had been recycled, probably dozens of times, over hundreds if not thousands of years. That strongly suggests a stagnant tech level."

"So what. So what!"

"And it didn't teleport its way to Antarctica, or use flying saucer antigravity. It fell with a parachute and a heat shield. And the isotope patterns in the casing tell us it was sent here using nuclear pulse propulsion, like the old *Project Orion* concept from the forties: Space travel by dropping nuclear bombs out the back hatch and setting them off. That means no warp drive. No wormholes. It's a 1.7-million-year-old machine and it's barely more advanced than the damned Space Shuttle. That leaves only two possibilities: either its creators bent over backwards to use *desperately* obsolete technology—"

"It's envy, isn't it?" you said. "You can't stand knowing you'll never accomplish close to what I have, and this is how—"

She spoke over you: "—or else Dandelion is as far as space flight technology *can* advance! If the speed of light is an unbreakable law—"

Your voice died in your throat, because there it was in her face now, behind the anger: the burst of epiphany you'd been waiting for all along. The ecstasy of a flawed paradigm giving way.

"—if there's no shortcut, then manned interstellar travel is a practical impossibility, no matter the technology. There are no viable energy sources between star systems and thus no way to sustain life at sub-light speeds, beyond keeping some germs warm with an RTG. And if that's true—"

Except it was corrupted: a perverse anti-epiphany that didn't kindle possibility but snuffed it out.

"—then there are no interstellar empires in the universe. No colonies. No Kardashev Scale. No ET will ever visit Earth. They all reach the same technological plateau and level off, indefinitely. They're all just . . . "

Stranded, you thought. Each confined to their own pitiful islands, never to set foot on another. The future that spread out before you was a fever-dream eternity of human beings—even as they continued to physically evolve over eons—driving the same cars to work and back again, wiling away evenings and weekends watching television and drinking beer until the last crushed can overflowed the trash; walking it out to the curb and glancing up at the glittering stars, and wondering only in passing what secrets they held, but never finding out, until the sun burned down and died alone in the cosmic night.

No snowflake or raindrop has touched Victoria Valley in a thousand millennia. There's no flora or fauna in sight, not even lichen on the rocks: just an endless blank canvas of bone-dry sand and alien-shaped boulders. It's so cold and dry that even microbes struggle here; now and then a seal wanders in from the coast and its mummified corpse joins an open-air crypt spanning thousands of years.

It's hard not to see this desert as a metaphor for the land between star systems. There's nothing to eat or drink or burn for warmth. The sun sets and doesn't rise again for six months, and even in the daylight the only thing keeping my fingers from freezing off are the chemical hand warmers I packed in—like the RTG that kept Dandelion's canister of primordial ooze alive for however many centuries it took to reach us.

At a mere ten percent the speed of light, that's all you can do: Try to keep warm. Pray you reach the next glimmer of light before your last cell turns to stone.

Still, there's a beauty in this place I can't describe: not despite its lifelessness, but because of it. There's nowhere on Earth quite as dead as here—yet it's no harder to see this place as the end of the world, as a world yet to begin.

The summer before you died, I took you down to the same beach where you and Margaret had once walked. We got ice cream from a stall on the waterfront, and when I looked back you were leaning out of your wheelchair. I had to run for the handles before you tipped over.

"What is it? You okay?"

You groaned and kept groping for the weed growing up between the sidewalk tiles, so I knelt and picked it for you. You turned the seed head carefully before your eyes, lost in thought.

"Making a wish?" I asked.

You crushed the dandelion, mashing it between your palms until it was only a pea-sized lump of pale fuzz.

"Without the stars we are doomed," you said, and your words haunted me—because even though I couldn't yet make any sense of them, I knew then that you and my mother weren't opposites but two sides of a coin.

Even when your mind was still sharp, you told yourself that Plateau Theory was merely her plot to betray you—but there were things you never knew. For all the scientific delight you once shared, she never trusted you enough to tell you about her breakdown. She never told you she'd watched the world end.

A decade before she joined the Project, the Agency had had her teaching computers to recognize the gamma ray signatures of nuclear blasts. A handful of times the job took her into the subterranean compartments of NORAD facilities—and on the last of those times, in the middle of a line of code, the sound of alarms turned her head to the sight of vault doors pivoting shut. She stumbled into the control room and her unspoken questions were answered by panicked shouts and missile trajectory maps whose eye-searing light reflected in spilled coffee, sweat-greased faces, hands that clenched telephones or prayed over radar images.

The screens said the first bombs would fall in 18 minutes. They said every American city would be ash within an hour.

There were many things that flashed before my mother's eyes, besides her life, as she sank back against the wall. She saw in every arc of neon the wicked transfiguration of a rocket meant to carry us to the stars. She saw in those lines of burning light an unholy vision of all humanity's genius bent back on itself, its space age dreams raining down to sterilize the whole world in nuclear fire.

Then somebody was helping her up, telling her it had all been a false alarm. A simulation tape loaded into a live computer. These things happen, they said. As if that helped.

Weeks passed before she could sleep again—and when she finally did, and when she woke, it was not into the world she'd known before. Suddenly the real was no longer merely a stepping stone to the possible.

The real was all there was.

• • •

I was born a little over nine months after Margaret submitted her report. By then the Project had been canceled. She'd moved to Livermore to spend her days with the bombs that filled her nightmares, and you and anyone else who'd stuck it out since the sixties had retired. You watched helplessly when they laid Dandelion in a lead casket and sent it down the salt mine shaft—no longer to safeguard its technology, so much as to spare the American public from wrestling with its philosophical implications.

You and my mother kept up an uneasy peace for most of my childhood. You developed elaborate ways of dismissing Plateau Theory (confining them to the safety of your journal). You found reasons to blame the Agency instead of her. I like to think I brought you some solace too.

You were as old as I am now, and I was five, the day you set me on my own path. I was poking at my plastic solar system placemat, tracing the concentric rings of orbits until I reached the outermost. That one was conspicuously wide and tilted away from the others.

"That's the planet Pluto," you said.

All the other planets hung over my bed on wires and string, but this one wasn't in the set. I'd never seen a photograph. I asked "What's it like?"

"Nobody knows! It's too far away to see. Even with the most powerful telescope there is."

"Cold," my mother said from another room. "Airless. Just craters and darkness."

You leaned in close, so she couldn't hear. You smiled knowingly and said "Maybe. Probably. But . . . what if?"

Twenty years later, we saw it through New Horizon's eyes: A world of plains and mountains and glaciers, circled by five moons, wrapped in an atmosphere that sublimates and condenses over centuries. It was a system unto itself, stranger and more beautiful than I could have imagined. By then I was well on my way.

The peace you'd made with Margaret was the first thing dementia took. It started with a few uncharacteristically vicious remarks. Out of nowhere you would stare at her with a look colder than the wind I'm tasting now. You picked fights over nothing. The more you forgot, the hotter your increasingly distorted memory of the Project's cancellation seemed to burn—and the rest of us were left to remember Thanksgiving 2004, when you hurled a saucer and shouted "Faster than light!" as it exploded against the dining room wall.

We couldn't reason with the personality changes. We never found a medication that helped. Whatever progress we made by talking about it was quickly erased. All we knew was that whatever rage had taken hold in you only seemed to apply to my mother, so from then on I was the one who went in alone to visit you and see to the practical concerns of your last years on Earth. I tried to be the proxy for the love she continued to hold for you. Sometimes I felt like a robotic probe sent somewhere too distant and hazardous for its maker.

For years we did this. I'd bring you out to the waterfront and enunciate the headlines until you heard them right, and you'd tell me my hair was too short for a girl, or the wrong color. I knew nothing of Dandelion.

One day I told you I was leaving for college. You asked what I was going to study, and I told you my plan to build probes for NASA. I'd said it a dozen times before, but that was the time you heard me. It seemed to freeze you solid.

You held my wrist and wept.

You couldn't tell me why. You couldn't remember all you needed to say. It took all your strength just to hold the thought, but you insisted there was something under your mattress that you needed to give me, and you didn't relent until all your old journals were in my hands. Then I put the sheets back on and helped you lie down, for what turned out to be the last time.

It was through your journals that I learned my mother had been a different person before I met her, though I didn't think I'd ever know that person. Every time I came home to visit, she'd only withdrawn further into herself. Her grief changed in shape and texture over the years, but it haunted every room of the house like the tingle of radiation.

The cancer diagnosis came in 2019, a few months before she was set to retire. It turned out to be operable—she would go into remission and live well for another twenty-two years—but it wrecked us both for a while. I took a leave from work to help her recover from the surgery, and we ended up sitting on that same haunted beach, watching the sun sink between the now-abandoned oil rigs. We barely shared a word until well into twilight.

"When I started, when I had you," she said, "my job was decommissioning warheads. I figured that was a good way to make myself useful."

Since we'll only ever have this one planet, she left unsaid. She closed her eyes and sighed sharply. I put my hand on her knee and she held it.

"The fuckers put me to work building new ones," she continued. "They're growing the stockpile for the first time since the Berlin Wall fell, and I went along with it. I had my pension to think about. But if one of those bombs ever gets used on people, I . . . . "

She choked on her words. The black waves lapped half-heartedly at the shore.

"Everything is falling apart," she said. "The world goes more to hell each day and it's hard to imagine anything stopping it. Nobody knows how to imagine that anymore."

"Ever heard of Nuclear Pulse propulsion?" I asked. "Accelerate a spacecraft by throwing nukes out the back door and setting them off, basically. It sounds absurd, but it works. In theory, I mean. We could use it to build an interstellar probe using present-day technology. Coincidentally, it's a good way to get rid of a lot of nukes."

She stared out to sea and nodded. "Too bad it would be extremely expensive. No political will for something like that."

"Not yet," I conceded. "But suppose something came along to change the dialogue. Maybe if some secrets were leaked. Something that could change everyone's perspective on humankind's place in the universe."

She didn't seem surprised that I knew about Dandelion. She didn't visibly respond at all. Finally she snorted and said "It's too dangerous to even talk about."

I sighed and stared out into the last light.

She added: "It's much too dangerous . . . to keep digital copies of all the Project's files and records on backup drives hidden throughout the house. And yet."

I started to laugh, but her grip on my hand tightened, a warning.

"Are we really going to do this?" she whispered.

I couldn't answer lightly. Beyond the threat that it would end my career and land both of us in prison, there was no way to know all the consequences of exposing Dandelion to the world. I knew people would wrestle with it in ways I couldn't hope to foresee, some of which I might regret. But I felt a very particular kind of optimism when I answered.

For years I had fallen into the trap of thinking of the relationship between your theories and hers as a battle between hope and despair. I wanted to believe that she was wrong and you were right: that the speed of light is a law meant to be broken, and the stars would be within our grasp any day. I clung to that desire even as microprocessors stopped getting smaller; even when our one attempt to inhabit Mars was vanquished by chronic illness and billowing dust; even as fusion power stubbornly refused to become viable.

Maybe the Plateau is real. Maybe we're already approaching the end of technological history. I gave years of my life to denial and bargaining and anger, and I've searched for counter-evidence in every way I know how. If it's there to find, I doubt I'll live to see it.

But along the way I found something else—something I would give anything to share with you, grandmother. Because I like to think that if only you'd been able to push through all your fear and disappointment and betrayal, you might have gotten around to realizing that if all the technology to build Dandelion already existed, it meant we could build our own.

The radio on my belt crackles and I know my time here is almost up. Soon I'll hear the helicopter blades coming to lift me out of this place: back to McMurdo Station, back into my wife's arms, and on to the first of several planes that will return us to California.

As we move North we'll exit the Antarctic Summer. The endless day will turn back to night—but the darkness that falls will reveal a light, brighter now than any star, in the final stages of its decades-long assembly.

You had only one child, and she had only me, and I won't be having any of my own. One of these days our part of this story will be finished—but if it ever gets me down, all I have to do is look up to see the next chapter being written. Its words are the DNA in 400 canisters of primordial ooze, each one swaddled in the warmth of isotopic decay: a 5,000-ton spiky ball of potential biospheres, soon to ride half the Earth's decommissioned nuclear arsenal across hundreds of lightyears of interstellar space, bound for proto-planetary disks.

Sometimes I like to imagine that the people (by any other name) who built Dandelion were copying a design given to them by their own forerunners, and so on, back to the beginning, whenever and wherever that was. I imagine that someone or something will one day feel the ghost of my palm from the other side of a sheet of American-made beryllium alloy.

I'll be a billion years dead by then. But before that, some Spring evening, I'll be watching the light of my life's work, and yours, and hers, fading into the black—and I'll be sitting on the beach where the sidewalk used to be with a fuzzy seed head in my hand, breathing deep to cast my wish.

ABOUT THE AUTHOR

Elly Bangs once rode her bicycle alone from Seattle to the Panama Canal. Now she lives in the former, fixing machines and writing novels. Her short fiction has appeared or is forthcoming in *Galaxy's Edge, Daily Science Fiction, Strange Horizons,* and anthologies such as *Bikes In Space* and *The Working Zealot's Guide to Gaining Capital in Pre-Apocalyptic America.* She is a graduate of Clarion West 2017.

The Foodie Federation's Dinosaur Farm

LUO LONGXIANG TRANSLATED BY ANDY DUDAK

1

A Lei was a young worker at the 045 Meat Union factory on Continent Three in starship Rhea. When the dinosaur uprising overwhelmed the factory, he used a hunting rifle to drop two great beasts that got in his way. He climbed over their corpses and fled deeper into the factory, toward the shuttle launch silos—but he was too late. The six shuttles were gone. Only their exhaust remained, suffusing the air.

A Lei shouted a torrent of abuse at his faithless coworkers. The racket of a collapsing assembly line drowned out his obscenities. A dinosaur more than five meters long jumped in front of him. He fired his rifle from the hip, but the creature nimbly evaded. The shot pierced a cooling pipe, and liquid nitrogen sprayed in torrents of white mist. The dinosaur's movements slowed. A Lei squeezed the trigger again, but nothing happened. He was out of ammo. He abandoned the weapon, turned, and fled.

He squeezed between two silos, the gap only a meter wide and about fifteen deep. This nook had survived countless launch-shock waves, never collapsing. It would temporarily shelter him from this dinosaur sneak attack. Now he needed a weapon, but all he found was canned dinosaur meat scattered about. He had no choice but to snatch a few cans. It was better than being empty-handed.

A pair of lantern-like eyes appeared at the gap entrance. The crimson eyes fixed on A Lei, making his scalp tingle, and heavy breathing filled his ears. The beast struck at a silo wall, long mouth clamping down, sharp teeth piercing, and a metal wall plate came off with the sound of a gunshot. A monstrous tooth landed near A Lei's foot. The canine, as long as his hand, stank of blood and made him retch.

The monster withdrew a few steps, swaying its large head. It peered into the gap at A Lei, seemingly loathe to abandon him. He saw it clearly now: a *draconis sapiens* over five meters long, from the largest-bodied dromaeosauridae branch, fast and deadly, cousin to the famous velociraptor, but with a much higher IQ. Some had brain volumes comparable to humans. They set traps and imitated other species to attract prey. Some witnesses claimed they emulated human tool use, and even parroted human speech. This was the most dangerous species of dinosaur. Almost every time livestock rebelled, dracopiens were involved. Their delicious flesh was widely known. At every supermarket counter in the Starship Alliance, dracopien was the most popular meat. Their weighty brains were used to make Dragon Brain Soup, a delicacy to rival Shark Fin or Swallow's Nest.

This dracopien wore a fine necklet. The inlaid nameplate identified its master, the researcher Ai Li-ke, and below that the creature's name, Steel Teeth.

It turned and moved off, seeming to give up. A Lei's sigh of relief was cut short when the monster picked up a hoisting jack and returned. It placed the jack in the gap and leisurely cranked, widening the entrance, metal squealing and giving way.

A Lei grew desperate and shouted, "Don't bother! I'm just skin and bones, not tasty at all!"

Steel Teeth's throat rumbled ominously. In crude tones it said, "I just ate a few. Humans really do taste awful. And I am full. That is not why I am doing this. It is exercise. Is that not a good enough reason?"

It wasn't surprising that this dracopien could talk. In addition to its developed brain and formidable intelligence, its larynx anatomy closely resembled a parrot's.

It showed no sign of stopping with the jack. A Lei's fight-or-flight impulse kicked in. He made his way into a deeper, narrower place. "So you're full," he said, squeezing in. "We might as well sit down and chat. Maybe even make friends?"

Steel Teeth's strength was extraordinary. After the jack had done its work, the monster bit its way forward, as if burning excess vigor, tearing away pipes and wires, clawing apart metal plating. A Lei crawled further in, frantic and ratlike, relying on memory to seek the butchering-mecha storage facility.

He crawled out of a ruptured industrial runoff pipe. Less than three meters away reclined a mecha suit, a butchering model about the size of a dracopien. The cockpit was open. The suit, which might have held its own against a T.Rex, had been abandoned. He had no time for this mystery. Rousing his courage, he took a deep breath and charged toward the armor. The foul stench of industrial runoff was like a chemical weapon, nearly overwhelming him. He covered his nose and reached for the mecha.

The runoff pipe was trampled flat with a thunderous crash. Steel Teeth's talons stabbed the floor right in front of A Lei. They could disembowel a T.Rex, and they'd come centimeters from tearing open his throat. Steel Teeth was like a cat toying with a mouse. Such a nimble killing machine couldn't miss like that. If it wanted A Lei dead, he'd already be slashed to ribbons.

A primal ferocity stirred in A Lei's heart. He dove into the cockpit. An impact rocked the canopy, Steel Teeth's claw a step late, screeching across the transparent shell. A Lei was soaked in cold sweat. He'd nearly been decapitated.

Now ensconced in the mecha, A Lei felt a dangerous pride. To suppress dinosaur uprisings, many mecha packed serious firepower, six-barrel Gatling machine cannons. He pulled a joystick. The mecha shivered, stood, extended manipulator arms toward the dracopien. Panels opened on the arms. A Lei cackled in his pride, eager to blow Steel Teeth to pieces.

But his smile froze.

His new arms were not sprouting cannons like he'd hoped. Instead, meter-long soup ladles emerged. He threw switches, retracting the ladles, extending giant tongs. A Lei stared, dumbfounded, switching tools in a frenzy. Forks, hooks, egg whisks, and other implements came up in succession, like a rotating lantern-carousel of paper horses. Against all reason, there was nothing like a useful weapon. Steel Teeth saw his frustration and collapsed with hissing laughter. "You foolish thing!" it said. "If this mecha had weapons, why would its former master have abandoned it?"

A Lei saw his chance and took it. He drove the mecha, trampling over the prone dinosaur and charged at a window. He smashed through, leaping out of the 045 Meat Union factory. Then he was falling, crashing through canopies of massive treelike ferns, more than twenty meters down, and into flea-bitten mud.

2

The Starship Alliance was nicknamed "The Foodie Federation" because its citizens had long ago grown dissatisfied with dull, flavorless foodstuffs synthesized in labs. Like their distant ancestors, they craved natural, pollution-free food, meat from species that grazed over vast territories, organically. The foodies were insatiable. They wanted exquisite variety, minced delicacies, food that took ten or even a hundred times more energy to raise and prepare than it provided. Such uneconomical practices were rare among nomadic space civilizations. To feed their strange addiction, the foodies constructed specialized agricultural starships. These immense man-made worlds provided grazing land, artificial sunlight, fertile soil, whole biospheres in the service of the foodies' appetite. All kinds of crops and livestock were raised, under natural Earthlike conditions. The yield was harvested or slaughtered after maturation, sent by freighter to every starship with megacities, to restaurants and supermarkets, meeting the demands of countless gluttons.

A few hundred years ago, the Starship Alliance returned to its origin world, Earth, seeking the fragments of its ancestral civilization. They took nearly everything of value from the ruins: cultural relics, dilapidated landmarks, specimens of flora and fauna, and fossils of extinct organisms. The dinosaur fossil payload came to megatons, and included many previously undiscovered species. Among the latter was the astonishing *draconis sapiens*.

Biologists conceived an idea: create a starship with a Cretaceous Earth habitat, resurrect paleo-organisms, including dinosaurs, so as to research the era. But the cost of the project would be massive. It wasn't easy to persuade stingy legislators to allocate funds, but after many rejections, they found someone who was interested.

"Just leave it to me," said the Venerable Madam Zheng Qingyin, president of the Alliance Foodstuffs Federation—in business circles known as Grandma Foodie—leaning on her dragon head cane in the Bio Research Institute's paleo-organism department.

An astonishing foodie carnival was staged at that year's congressional budget conference. AFF freighters crowded the Congressional Plaza. "Distinctive Prehistoric Delicacies" were handed out, free of charge. AFF-owned celebrities performed on stage. Billboards shouted slogans:

"Make any dinner table more sumptuous!"

"T.Rex leg burgers, steamed diplodocus, savory and spicy pterosaur wings!"

"Take your place at the Starship Alliance's luxurious banquet table!"

The Venerable Madam Zheng, white-haired, ruddy-complexioned, hale and hearty, walked with vigorous strides into the Capitol Building, deploying her dragon head cane to great dramatic effect. She carried a draft resolution in her other hand. She didn't use lengthy speeches to subjugate the legislators. Instead, she made sure they each had samples of dinosaur meat to try. When the few vegetarian legislators furrowed their brows and refused, she tantalized them with an equally delicious ancient pteridophyte banquet.

The Capitol Building had become a mansion of delicacies.

"I won't lecture you," the Venerable Madam said, "on the importance of a diverse diet to human well-being. There's no need, am I right?"

Her scientists were arrayed behind her, ready to hold forth on the topic for months, if called upon. She'd prepared truckloads of technical data on the proposed starship and its Cretaceous habitat. Its cost would dwarf that of traditional agricultural ships. It would allow biologists to research extinct life, but of course this was really about the foodies, and eating.

She got through the proposal effortlessly. When she emerged at the top of the Capitol steps, smiling and satisfied, a multitude of gluttons erupted with applause. Alliance TV broadcasted everything. The Venerable Madam had been wild in her youth. Now she felt that old wantonness return. Raising her dragon head cane, she cried, "Our slogan is . . . !"

The crowded square gave its booming reply: "Eat everything on two legs except people! Eat everything on four legs except stools!"

Building the new starship would take over a hundred years. Grandma Foodie Zheng Qingyin wouldn't live to see it completed, but her draft resolution would profoundly change the Starship Alliance dining table. After DNA fragments had been extracted, and paleo-organisms were coming back to life species by species, scientists noted that dracopiens were intelligent organisms. There was extensive debate: the resurrection of a dinosaur with human-equivalent IQ was no small matter. But in the end, the foodies' argument was simple and persuasive: Are dracopiens delicious? If so, resurrect!

3

The Cretaceous habitat was wildly unsuitable for humans. The world outside the factories was verdant, a wetland teeming with reptiles. People accidentally stepped on crocodiles and other beasts quite often. Dense fern canopies blotted out sky and sun. This primeval forest was bathed in a luxuriant mist, and the air, at over forty Celsius, was suffocating. It was like being in a giant food steamer. The pteridophyte fauna, lacking the structure and root systems of woody plants, needed the moist surroundings to survive. Some of the treelike ferns reached thirty meters tall. This world was so saturated that living people could molder.

A Lei made his mecha sit up. Luckily the interior was climate controlled, or he would already have been steam-cooked by the atmosphere. He hadn't driven a few steps before the mecha slipped into a bog, and he had to get upright again, this time with difficulty. This factory mecha was not suited to Cretaceous mud.

A Lei glanced back at the factory, which resembled a massive spider, several hundred meters wide, lying sprawled upon the earth. Normally it advanced like a bulldozer, gobbling up fern forest. Ground effect vehicles, like great dragonflies, would be dispatched from their tarmac on the roof, and in great swarms hunt dinosaurs. The conveyor belts would hurtle forward continuously, processing all kinds of dinosaur meat products. There were many of these roving factories in starship Rhea. The fern forests grew fast and weed-like in the warm, moist environment, and could be harvested regularly. The tender pteridophytes were rich in carbohydrates and protein. Most of a pteridophyte was edible, unlike flowering plants with their limited offerings of fruits, seeds, and certain leaves. The stunningly fast growth of Cretaceous flora was a clear demonstration to scientists of how the colossi, the dinosaurs, had been fed. Gourmands were pleasantly surprised at how fast the dinosaurs reproduced in this blistering climate—so much for the assumption of slow reptilian birthrates. Brood after enormous brood, breeding faster than rats: it turned out that Rhea was twice as productive as traditional agricultural starships. It seemed dinosaurs wouldn't have to be domesticated. Hunting was sufficient.

As A Lei carefully observed his surroundings, Steel Teeth rushed down the nearly-vertical factory wall and dashed across fern roots and muck, leaving no trace. A Lei was reminded of its awful cousin, the swift and violent velociraptor, and he failed to react. It felt like a hundred-ton truck hit him. His mecha was like a kite with its string cut, airborne, beyond control, then crashing through tree-fern saplings—and finally, mecha-face down in the mire.

Steel Teeth's talons pressed down on the machine. Its teeth scraped, seeking purchase, but it couldn't get the cockpit open. It gave up grudgingly. A Lei came to, feeling like all his bones had been shattered. Luckily, he'd landed in spongy marshland. If it had been solid stone, he might have been crushed inside the mecha.

Steel Teeth had been slower in the factory, where it was 20 or so degrees Celsius. Although dinosaurs were considered warm blooded, their capacity for body temperature regulation was inferior to that of mammals and birds. Out here in the damp heat, at over 40 degrees, it was ideal dinosaur weather. Below 10 degrees, most dinosaurs lost their mobility, or even died en masse.

A Lei sat the mecha up, and again Steel Teeth knocked it down. A Lei raised both hands and said, "Okay buddy. We're both intelligent creatures. How about we sit down for a nice chat?"

"Okay," Steel Teeth replied. It was at its wit's end, after all. The mecha was a conundrum. The last attack had consumed the dinosaur's strength, and it needed a rest, just like A Lei. It sat down much like a hen, stomach to the ground. The dinosaur kinship with birds was plain.

"You seem familiar with humans," A Lei said. "Surely you were raised and trained by someone . . . "

The creature said, "My foster father Ai Li-ke was a researcher of extinct life, living in solitude. He gave me human knowledge."

"And what happened to him?"

Steel Teeth laughed, displaying its keen incisors. "He was not very good. His meat was old. Too many bones. Hurt my teeth."

A Lei was shocked. "You ate him?"

"Humans have strange defects," Steel Teeth said. "You like domesticating house pets, believing you can imbue them with human feelings and reason. With dogs, horses, and other such social animals, long domestication can render them docile. But as for solitary animals . . . no matter how good you are to me, good enough to make me see you as kin, well, one mountain cannot brook two tigers. And we kill our own kind. The mother snake lays a brood and then just leaves. The eggs hatch and the young must fend for themselves. There is no familial emotion or attachment in the snake brain, no sense of friendship. How can you domesticate that? Change fundamental brain structure? No matter how good you are to creatures like us, we only see you as prey."

This great reptile's words resonated with A Lei. It seemed the dracopien, for all its mental development, was no more affectionate or friendly than a snake. A Lei said, "I've never met such a wise and farsighted dinosaur."

"Thank you," Steel Teeth said, lying prostrate on the ground. "You can call me Mister Wise and Farsighted Crouching Dragon."

4

Getting rid of this dracopien wasn't going to be easy. It became clear to A Lei as he watched the beast kill a T.Rex. Steel Teeth cleverly enraged its prey, luring the massive creature into soft mud, where it became stuck, and the hunter easily prevailed.

"I don't understand," A Lei said. "Your kind is quite rare, for a late Cretaceous apex predator. We've found so many T.Rex fossils, but few dracopien fossils. Actually, we found none until the SA returned to Earth."

Steel Teeth bit off a chunk of T.Rex flesh and devoured it. "We dracopiens do not lay many eggs. And we like to kill each other, so our numbers are naturally low. But, I have a dream. I see a great dinosaur civilization. I see dracopiens destroying humanity, and replacing it."

A dinosaur with a dream: this was a day of firsts for A Lei. He chose to dampen the creature's enthusiasm: "Establishing a civilization isn't easy. Mastering fire would be step one. We've never found a trace of fire production from the dinosaur age. Can you friction-drill?"

Steel Teeth lifted its head and gazed about. The dense fern forest hid much of the sky, while enveloping fog made a salted egg yoke of the westering sun. The dracopien leapt up, and came down on a tree fern, smashing it to the ground. It seized half the trunk in its mouth and flung it before A Lei. "Drill for fire?" it said, in a rage. "With this saturated fern material, in this saturated world, show me fire-drilling! Suirenshi, last of the Three August Ones, legendary inventor of fire, would be at his wit's end in this place!"

A Lei had stepped on Steel Teeth's tail with this problem of fire. Lack of fire production was dinosaur evolution's biggest flaw. Humans had come into the universe a mere three-million years ago, while *draconis sapiens,* from birth to asteroid strike, may have been around a good deal longer, yet never mastered flame. They never expanded their food options with cooking, or smelted metal, or created advanced tools. There had never been a dinosaur civilization.

A Lei's stomach growled as he sat in the cockpit and watched Steel Teeth gorge itself.

He drove the mecha, stepping away, but the beast leapt and knocked him down. After several thwarted attempts, A Lei knew he was trapped. He was meant to starve here. "You said your dream was to replace us," he said. "But do you understand human civilization?"

"I understand a bit," it said. "We have gathered much data on humans."

"And you comprehend it all?"

The beast cocked its head. "Most of it . . . no."

"Then you shouldn't have eaten your foster father. He would have been happy to help, I imagine."

"Just so. I immediately regretted it, after devouring him."

A Lei finally understood. A dracopien's appetite overrode its rational faculty. Having eaten its fill, reason returned. When its belly growled, it became an unthinking, ferocious beast. A Lei saw an opportunity. "You must be in dire need of someone who understands human civilization. If I may be so bold, I could fill that role. I could help you decipher what you mean to annihilate."

Steel Teeth returned to the factory and went inside. It soon returned, carrying a flamethrower. It was impossible to friction-drill in this moist world, but a flamethrower was another matter. A Lei watched the dracopien roast the T.Rex meat, puzzled. This sort of carnivore didn't normally like cooked meat.

Steel Teeth tossed a well-done T.Rex leg in front of the mecha. It opened its bloody, fearsome mouth and said, "You are welcome to join us."

"Us? There are others?" A Lei cautiously opened the canopy as the mecha forked a fragrant chunk of meat and brought it up.

Steel Teeth looked up and gave a long, ominous roar that made the ground tremble. Moments later, a group of dracopiens emerged into view. Steel Teeth extended its arms and said, "Welcome to the Steel Teeth tribe."

5

The dracopiens had always tried to imitate human civilization. Rhea employees talked about this often enough.

A Lei came to the so-called Steel Teeth tribe's home, a simple, crude structure hidden between a mountain range and a river. On the doorway was an upside-down sign: "Ai Li-ke, Research Facility." Steel Teeth had seized the place and turned it into a fortress. The surrounding area was piled with hewn-down tree ferns. It seemed the dracopiens had meant to build a stockade with them, but they'd found the material too flexible and abandoned the project. They'd hunted down large dinosaur skeletons instead, using a mixture of stone and bone to construct a gruesome and intimidating city wall.

A Lei knew that primitive human tribes had built enclosing walls to repel wild beast incursions. He didn't understand why apex predators like dracopiens needed such protection. Perhaps they were just imitating human behavior. Tree fern shanties stood here and there between the wall and the lab, a solemn little primeval town. The dracopiens had learned the human concept of shelter, but not human construction standards. The shacks were made of broad tree fern stalks and leaves. The roofs were slapdash, barely qualifying as shelter. Still, these dracopiens were far more advanced than other dinosaurs. Some gathered in front of huts to polish hunting implements. From a technological perspective, the tools were close to human Neolithic level, but they weren't made of stone. Discarded human machine parts served instead—machine arms from dismantled factories, iron pipes, and the like, all ground down to points and made into javelins, lances, and other primitive weapons.

There were many such primitive tribes in starship Rhea. Although Cretaceous era dracopiens had humanlike IQs, they'd never entered the tribal era on Earth. These tribes in Rhea had clearly resulted from human influence. All kinds of plundered posters covered the fort, many of them SA city scenes, or steampunk-style space factories, and wide shots of spacecraft swarms like stellar multitudes. But most were illustrations of delicacies from various SA regions. On each of these, a graffito had been scrawled, in characters like roaches crawling across the image: "Our goal is a sea of food!"

"I thought your goal was to destroy human civilization," A Lei said, "to remove and replace us."

"Just so, but our ultimate goal is to eat. Humanity has many tasty delicacies. My foster father used to share them with me, fine foods from other starships, even from alien civilizations. For the sake of gourmet dining, humans have spanned thousands of lightyears, and returned to Earth to excavate fossils. You made this Cretaceous environment, this high-quality grazing land . . . the audacity! Foodies are the most powerful force in the universe. If we conquer humanity, all that wonderful food will be ours!"

In the final analysis, these dracopiens were mouth-straight-to-heart foodies. Steel Teeth did nothing to conceal its yearning. A Lei hadn't expected these primitive dracopiens to be pursuing something higher than mere destruction.

Entering the stronghold, he saw most of the lab instruments had been demolished for weapon parts. Books lay scattered on the floor, most of them rotted by the climate. The few intact volumes were ancient human histories.

"They say humans progressed from primitive tribes to tribal coalitions," Steel Teeth explained. "On that foundation they established nations. Before we establish our own great tribal alliance, the latter part of human history is useless to us."

These fragmentary histories outlined tribal warfare in remote human ages. Steel Teeth said, "We have run into a bit of a problem."

"What's that?"

"I threw away all the weapons materiel Foster Father left to me. At the time, I believed they could not compare with sharp teeth. But during our battles with the tribe on the other side of the river, their flame catapults were ferocious. We suffered grievous losses."

"That's why you attacked the factory?" A Lei said. "To find better weapons?"

Steel Teeth led A Lei outside, to a captured enemy catapult. Made of fern tree, and using oil rendered from dinosaur fat, it was a crude machine. Its only real virtue was the human-made flamethrower lashed to it, which lit the dino-oil payloads. A Lei, staring at Steel Teeth's deadly incisors, said, "You should learn to peacefully coexist. You're all dracopiens. Infighting is pointless."

"Enough of that useless rubbish!" Steel Teeth said. "In ancient times did you humans not make rivers of blood? Without big and powerful tribal alliances, would human civilization have been possible? Did not those powerful human war chiefs, like Odin or Emperor Yan, become deities worshipped by later generations? Does your Starship Alliance not have a battleship named the Emperor Yan?"

These dracopiens were naturally despotic. A Lei worried about debating and infuriating Steel Teeth. The prudent choice was to shut up.

Steel Teeth went vigorously about its leadership duties, handling tribal affairs big and small. It delegated a host of technological problems to A Lei. Luckily, these dracopien tech issues were of the simple Neolithic variety: find abandoned human metal fit for weaponry, develop new techniques for making sharper arrows, learn how to fling fire in this moist environment, and how to process tree fern material into something harder and wood-like.

When he knew he was unobserved, A Lei relaxed and breathed in the mecha. He wanted to contact headquarters, but didn't know how. Despairing, he glanced down, and saw a hand device on the floor of the cockpit. It must have been dropped by the previous pilot. A Lei smacked himself upside the head in a fierce self-rebuke. If he'd seen the device earlier and called for help, he might have avoided his current predicament.

6

He huddled in the cockpit with the device in his hands. His trembling finger entered the wrong number several times, but he finally connected to the 045 Meat Union factory assistant director's office. "Director!" he shouted. "It's A Lei! I'm trapped in Rhea!"

"A Lei?" The assistant director sounded frightened. "You're still alive?"

"If not, who are you talking to?"

"We all assumed you'd been eaten, so we didn't arrange a rescue team. But on the bright side, financial affairs offered their condolences. They paid for the funeral, and the accidental death insurance has paid out to your parents. Quite a sum!"

A Lei had to stop himself from smashing the hand device. "So my family's quite happy with everything then? You were worried about further losses if you dispatched rescue, is that it? Why eat more financial loss when you can just write me off? Well let me tell you . . . you've got bigger problems. These dracopiens aren't merely lashing out at the factory. They're conspiring to revolt. They mean to establish a huge tribal coalition. They want to overthrow human civilization and replace it. We need to sound the alarm. Better yet, we need to report this to SA government. We need the Marines if we're going to suppress these fucking lizards!"

"So you want to smash everyone's rice bowls," the assistant director said, growing incensed himself. "You know if Accidents and Safety inspects, all Union factories have to shut down and reorganize. What's everyone supposed to eat? The Northwest Wind? Now wait . . . if you're really saying the dracopiens are conspiring to overthrow humanity . . . Just hold on, I'll report it to the higher-ups and call you right back." The assistant director disconnected.

A few minutes later, the device buzzed in A Lei's hand, and he answered. An old, dignified voice came through, claiming to be the AFF executive director in charge of Rhea.

"Executive d-director." A Lei was low-level, a Union factory worker. He was talking to the man in charge of all food enterprises in Rhea.

"Young man," the old voice said, "tell me frankly . . . what's happening there?"

A Lei dared not hold anything back. He recounted the whole disaster, systematically and in full detail.

"That's quite a story," the old man said. "You're sure my friend Ai Li-ke was eaten?"

"Y-yes."

The old man sighed. "No wonder I haven't heard from him in so long. Ai Li-ke was an outstanding researcher for us. He played an important role in constructing the dinosaur pasturelands. And he was a skilled cook! Specialized in dinosaur eggs. Do you have anything of his? Keepsakes? If so, bring them back to me, and I'll reward you well."

A Lei sifted through the materials he'd collected. "There's only fragments of his notebooks left, and a few memory chips. Sir, you must think of a way to rescue me from Rhea. Otherwise I have no way of getting this stuff to you." He had to prioritize his own little life.

"You're sitting in a mecha now?"

"Of course. Otherwise I'd have been eaten."

"So it would seem the dracopiens also don't know what to do with you. You have two options . . . sound the alarm and report to the police, getting a rescue team dispatched. That's the safest way, but you'd be letting a once-in-a-lifetime opportunity slip through your fingers."

That cut through A Lei's fear. "And the other option?"

"Cut a bloody path out of there, escape on your own, and bring me Steel Teeth's head. You would have a hero's welcome, and a promotion. How does deputy captain of a hunting squad sound?"

A Lei did some quick mental calculations. "I'd be equal to an assistant factory director."

"Satisfactory?"

"Yes! Ten thousand times yes! If you'll keep your promise . . . " He could struggle half a lifetime and never climb that high. He grinned, seeing money, glittering futures, his current danger forgotten.

After the old man had disconnected, A Lei sat there fantasizing. A grim voice like a thunderclap brought him back to the Cretaceous: "Who were you talking to?"

A Lei panicked. He'd forgotten that dinosaur hearing was far keener than his. Steel Teeth had probably heard the entire dialogue.

7

After that fateful call, A Lei spent every day in fear. Steel Teeth seemed to know its severed head was the price for a deputy captain throne. A group of fearsome dracopiens always watched him, and he was never alone with their chieftain. Sometimes he had to fight the urge to sound the alarm, but the lure of promotion always won out. Steel Teeth had him designing various weapons for the coming tribal wars. A Lei knew nothing of weapon design, but he knew how to research Stone Age weaponry on the hand device. In the course of one hectic month, he designed many weapons for the tribe.

A Lei understood well enough that if Steel Teeth really wanted him dead, there were many ways. It couldn't bite through the mecha, but it could starve him. It could slow-cook a stegosaurus leg right in front of him, wait for him to go mad with hunger and leave the cockpit, then casually devour him. But as long as A Lei produced weapon designs, it seemed Steel Teeth would refrain from harming him.

He was confined to the castle, but he heard dracopiens speaking of their chieftain's conquests. Steel Teeth was vanquishing tribe after tribe, consolidating power. He also heard the 045 Meat Union factory was back in business. No one seemed to care about one low-level worker's whereabouts.

It was getting harder to find new data for weapons designs. The decisive moment was fast approaching.

He brought up Steel Teeth's domestication record for the hundredth time, a series of videos shot by Ai Li-ke.

Dracopien reproduction was much like certain turtles'. Parental involvement ended when an egg was laid. Little dracopiens hatched ready to hunt. Like many fish, amphibian, and reptile species in times of scarcity, siblings devoured each other. When Ai Li-ke discovered Steel Teeth's nest, the little dracopiens were at war. Finally, just one hatchling remained. Ai prepared cow milk and chicken eggs for it, but the fierce little creature only snarled at its new benefactor. Ai Li-ke found this charming, and named it Steel Teeth.

A montage followed, Ai patiently teaching Steel Teeth to read. Raising this emotionless, reptilian thing was far more difficult than raising a mammal. Mammals come with emotional attachment software preinstalled. Much of the time, Ai had no choice but to administer electric shock to make little Steel Teeth learn obedience. The other method was feeding. Young Steel Teeth learned to curry favor with Ai in order to enjoy the great variety of human food. A sumptuous banquet flowed from Ai's hand, and Steel Teeth grew very fast, ending up much larger than a wild dracopien.

Naturally, Steel Teeth's knowledge far exceeded its wild cousins'. This, combined with its superior size and vigor, allowed it to easily defeat other dracopiens in combat. By the time Ai Li-ke was seventy, Steel Teeth had become the alpha of a large dracopien pack. Tribalism was something new for the species, a new world in which Steel Teeth was the grim hegemon.

In Steel Teeth's eyes, A Lei's usefulness was drawing to a close. One day it brought some trusted followers into the fortress, where A Lei was hard at work measuring a section of excavated tree fern rhizome, which was meant to become a mortar cannon. A Lei puzzled over two problems: how to produce and use gunpowder in this moist world, and how to make tree fern material strong enough to endure the force of discharge.

Rhea was, in the end, merely the human approximation of a Cretaceous environment. It differed from the real thing. To prevent flowering angiosperms from squeezing out pteridophytes, humans strove to eliminate higher plants from the ecosystem, not to mention maple, birch, and metasequoia. Thus, hard building materials were difficult to come by.

Steel Teeth brought a taloned foot down, smashing the nascent mortar to pieces. "Stop tinkering with such nonsense. This is not Earth. We have bypassed the Iron Age."

A Lei went pale. He knew he couldn't make a mortar. He'd been going through the motions of research, to keep death at bay. Now Steel Teeth had seen through this. He feared the moment of truth had come.

Steel Teeth's followers dragged the mecha toward a large gathering of dracopiens. A Lei was deposited on a massive, crude contrivance of tree fern, a kind of war chariot. Looking down upon the wide expanse of dracopiens, A Lei reckoned the alliance was now ten tribes strong. A solemn Steel Teeth reviewed its army. There were many other war chariots, lashed to domesticated stegosaurs and ceratopsians. A vanguard of dracopien-driven T.Rexes, armored in bone and teeth, rushed toward the battlefront.

"I have unified all the tribes of the Yellow River's north shore," Steel Teeth said to A Lei. "Today we unite with the south shore tribes, at long last. Behold, this world's highest lord."

Steel Teeth's "Yellow River" was the great waterway of the region. A hundred kilometers of dracopien deforestation had led to erosion, turning the river into a yellow, turbid flow. "If the name Yellow River gets around," A Lei said, "many Earthlings might have objections. Can you change it?"

Steel Teeth snorted. "The chief of the south shore alliance is named Chiyou, God of War."

"Really?" A Lei said in amazement.

"That is really my nickname for it."

This joke fell flat, but Steel Teeth's knowledge did more to kill any possible levity. It knew the hazards of a cross-river military campaign. It had chosen to launch its offensive in the enveloping fog of early morning, to obscure numbers and movement. A Lei noticed strange little vehicles among Steel Teeth's forces, tree fern constructions with crude but clever gears driven by the wheels. No matter which way they turned, their indicator rods always pointed across the river.

Steel Teeth's dracopiens were armed with metal weapons burnished by stone and bone. Garlands of some pteridophyte, blooming with primitive flowers, were bound to their heads. The plant was a favorite edible among dinosaurs, resembling Chinese cabbage. To A Lei these advancing dracopiens were comical, a group of hooligans with cabbage hats, but the Steel Teeth tribe knew what it was doing. The headdresses would distinguish friend from foe. If a dracopien emerged from the fog of war without one, it was an enemy, and must be put to the hatchet.

The campaign opened with a salvo of burning missiles, dinosaur oil and pteridophyte kindling bundled around large rocks and flung from catapults into the mist. The clamor of impacts and howling enemies traveled across the water. Dracopiens ignited torches bound to the tails of their T.Rex and stegosaur mounts, and drove these beasts charging toward the opposite bank. Many enemies were caught unawares, panicking in the fog, and were hewn down. As others took up arms, Steel Teeth's main force reached the south shore. With sharp claws and cold steel, they conducted a ruthless slaughter.

"I am very grateful to you," Steel Teeth said to a dumbstruck A Lei. "All your hard work has paid off. Now, I should send you back to your place of origin."

"You mean the Starship Alliance?"

Steel Teeth knocked the mecha prone. Several dracopiens poured dinosaur oil from fern leaf receptacles onto the mecha, and one used a factory flamethrower to ignite it. The mecha burst into flames, and A Lei realized the war chariot was actually a massive catapult. Steel Teeth slashed the restraining rope with a claw swipe, and A Lei, with his several tons of mecha, was airborne and trailing fire. He had become ammunition.

Steel Teeth watched him fly toward the far shore. "Godspeed," it said, "on the reincarnation road!"

8

This was the largest dinosaur conflict A Lei had ever seen. As he came to, his broken body shot through with pain, cockpit life support showed he'd been unconscious for two days. He had a broken rib, two broken legs, and the ground shook as immense dinosaurs clashed all around him, and on top of him, trampling the mecha as they vied for position. The machine was pounded into the riverbank marsh. Starving and dehydrated, he was forced to drink the foul water and dinosaur blood leaking through a crack in the cockpit. Most of the time he didn't dare to move, waiting, still and quiet, for the war to end. On the third day of this vigil, there was finally silence above. The dracopiens were no longer fighting at close quarters. He touched a joystick, and the mecha sat up. Dinosaur corpses lay piled all around. He stared in amazement. The Yellow River had been dyed red.

"Life is strong in you."

It was Steel Teeth, behind him. He turned to find the great warlord lying prone, and gravely wounded, on a burned-to-carbon catapult.

"I'm not strong. This mecha is. After all, it's a high-tech SA product. With a hundred-and-fifty-million-year technological lead, how can you lose?" Every word he spoke was a stab from his broken rib. Steel Teeth only heard him thanks to the brainwave converter in the cockpit, synthesizing speech and amplifying it.

"I have not lost," Steel Teeth said, "but neither have I won. This enemy chief was raised by a human, like me. It was big like me, knowledgeable like me. I nicknamed it Chi You in my desire to defeat it. A pity I am not the Yellow Emperor.[1] Chi You is dead, but I will soon follow it."

"Wait, you mean there are others like Ai Li-ke?"

Steel Teeth moved its massive head with great effort. "This was humanity's plan all along. Resurrect us, educate us, lure us toward humanlike development, toward tribes and alliances, toward building the foundation of a society through hand-to-hand combat. No intelligent species can resist trying to make a civilization, even if they know they are a moth darting toward a flame. How can we turn away from war? Every dracopien dreams of becoming an apex foodie. We dream like you dream. We want to make a world according to our desires. We long to satisfy our craving for endless, delicious variety."

"We humans don't just dream of food. We pursue higher things. Moreover, I plan to become a vegetarian." Watching tributaries of blood flow into the red river, A Lei thought he would never want meat again.

"Eating is always the first priority!" Steel Teeth growled. "All life must eat. Hunger is the eternal constant. No food means no life. No life means no dreams, no realization of dreams. Even a superintelligent species is, in the end, biological. Whether you eat animals or plants, you are eating living things. Humanity is just another living thing. Better to admit this. I see through your hypocritical compassion. It is pathetic."

A Lei walked the mecha over, meaning to stop Steel Teeth's bleeding. The beast lashed out, its great mouth ripping the already-cracked canopy to pieces. A Lei, now sitting unprotected in his much-abused machine, stared into a gaping mouthful of teeth, and said, "You don't want me to save you?"

"Why should I want that? And how can you save me? It is eat or be eaten, the primal law of the natural world. Plants devour inorganic matter and sunlight. Herbivores eat the plants, and carnivores eat the herbivores. Even high and mighty humans, apex predators that you are, must one day rot and become meal for plants. This is the way of things, the cycle. As intelligent life nurtured by the natural world, your duty is not to destroy this law of nature that brought you about, but rather to protect it. You humans created this world of Rhea. To we dracopiens, you are gods. Gods should preserve natural laws. Gods should maintain nature's balance, not destroy it."

A Lei was confused. "You revere humanity as gods, yet wish to replace us?"

Steel Teeth seemed to grin broadly. "We want to become gods ourselves, revered, with unlimited food! But this is impossible. Rhea is not old Earth. It is not free and unrestrained. There is no coal here, no oil, for industry. Even if humans allowed us to develop freely, we still could not establish a civilization comparable to yours. But we strive, nevertheless. We cannot even reach the Iron Age, but we strive, and lay down our lives without regret."

"I still don't understand. Why is humanity imparting knowledge to dracopiens?"

"For more delicious, higher-quality dining, and more developed brains. For your supermarkets and restaurants. For minced meat and Dragon Brain Soup! Foodies as discerning as humans are no longer satisfied with mere free-range meat. You crave carnivores that rush about and fight hand-to-hand. I thought you understood this."

A Lei contemplated Steel Teeth for a long time. "You're the most wise and farsighted foodie I've ever met."

Steel Teeth laughed, coughed up blood. Lying prone on the burned wreckage of the catapult, it said, "Please call me Mister Wise and Farsighted Crouching Dragon."

"I can't," A Lei said. "Zhuge Liang[2] might rise from the grave and sue for copyright infringement."

Steel Teeth's laugh was like quaking thunder. "Do not be ashamed of being a foodie. You humans have advanced far enough to break from the natural world, and you thrive. If you followed this timid, benevolent morality you speak of, and ate only foods synthesized in your labs, hundreds of starship biospheres would not exist. The countless animals depending on your pastureland habitats would not exist. We Cretaceous organisms would still be mere fossils. Dracopiens think this way . . . if humans do not eat it, it cannot possibly survive. Dracopiens have never resented your cultivation and hunting of our kind. You humans think so highly of yourselves, but your time will come. Are you not destined to become a feast for microorganisms and plants?"

A squad of ground effect vehicles appeared in the distance. Steel Teeth gave a mighty roar, and slowly rose. Wounds pouring blood, it faced A Lei in the unprotected cockpit.

"I have devoured much prey in this lifetime, but I never tormented my victims. My kills were swift, and I am proud of this. Humans brought us into this world, and we delighted in combat, to realize an impossible dream. We are born and have only a few dozen years, but that is enough. And now I tell you one last thing . . . respect your food. I know you mean to take my head and become a captain. We abide by the laws of nature. Let us see who shall eat, and who shall be eaten. Come now. Fight!"

This would be a fair duel. A Lei, his canopy gone, was no longer impervious to sword and spear, while Steel Teeth, with its injuries, was neither stronger nor faster than the mecha. Roaring, the dracopien lunged. A Lei touched a joystick. The only thing in the mecha's arm that might grudgingly be called a weapon—an oversized meat skewer—popped up. Steel Teeth's deadly bite clamped shut centimeters from A Lei's face. The skewer stabbed, sinking deep into Steel Teeth's heart.

"Thank you," A Lei said, "for teaching me wisdom, Wise and Farsighted Speaker."

"Please call me Mister Wise and Farsighted Crouching Dragon." Steel Teeth's lantern-like eyes slowly closed, the barest trace of regret marring its satisfaction.

9

When danger and opportunity coexist, courage is the key to deciding one's fate. If A Lei had chosen to raise the alarm, he would have remained a common worker. He would have spent his life in the stink of the 045 Meat Union factory, perhaps retiring before he could attain the career summit of foreman.

When he brought Steel Teeth's head back to the company, the hero's greeting left him dumbfounded. There was adulation and praise for this young person, so composed, so calm as he faced the lights and cameras, calm as a mountain. Only A Lei knew this was a façade. It was fear that kept him unmoving. After the uprising, the AFF needed a model hero to redeem its image. Despite his lack of qualifications, A Lei was decorated and adorned at the public relations department, and made into an optimal spokesperson.

At 22, A Lei became the youngest-ever deputy captain of a hunting squad. This promotion broke several rules, and he knew his qualifications and abilities were being discussed, and found wanting. The higher-ups wanted an experienced hunter. They were waiting for him to wash out. The smallest error could get him demoted, so he was cautious, devoted, and energetic in his work. He couldn't let this opportunity slip through his fingers.

He was very young for such a position. Most of the other deputy captains were of his parents' generation, and he was higher up than most of his contemporaries. After five years at the job, he got married and enjoyed conjugal bliss. He was promoted, step by step, and ended up the AFF executive director in charge of starship Rhea. By the time his career ended, there were more than a thousand others in the AFF of his rank: pasture habitat executive directors, farming colony planet managers, or exploration team chiefs seeking new foods throughout the cosmos. But A Lei never left Rhea.

For most of his life, A Lei sat upright in a tall building, watching his expanse of Cretaceous land, watching dracopiens clash in war after tribal war. Both humans and dracopiens knew what it was all about. Hunting dracopiens was still dangerous work, and although hunting squads were brave, hazarding their lives to kill all types of dinosaurs and deliver them to dining tables, dracopiens were the exception. Better to watch their battlefields, and wait, and harvest warriors on the verge of death. That was how you got the delicacy Dragon Brain Soup.

Many higher-ups in the hunting squads had dinosaur skulls decorating their offices, and A Lei was no exception. His massive dracopien skull had an engraved plaque beneath it: "Mister Wise and Farsighted Steel Teeth, a truth-speaking friend who changed my life."

Whenever he encountered problems, and felt irresolute, A Lei would swivel his chair and look up at Steel Teeth's skull. He tried to imagine how Steel Teeth, the determined warlord, would handle the thorny issue. A Lei's subordinates feared and respected him. They called him "master who thinks deep, like a dinosaur."

One day, A Lei sat in his office contemplating a dracopien egg he'd collected after a tribal war. Thinking of Steel Teeth, he began planning his retirement. He would hatch this egg, build a secluded house here in Rhea, and teach the little dinosaur Steel Teeth's wisdom. He would raise it to be the next generation's dracopien leader. After much thought concerning its name, he settled on Steel Teeth the Second.

Perhaps, someday, Steel Teeth the Second would eat him, as the First had eaten Ai Li-ke. Or perhaps it wouldn't be interested in human meat, and A Lei would die a natural death in Rhea, in the little house, and become food for bacteria and plants. Neither ending was bad, as far as a pious foodie was concerned.

FOOTNOTES

1 - The Yellow Emperor is one of the three legendary Chinese rulers and culture heroes. Often regarded as the originator of Chinese civilization, he is said to have defeated Chiyou, God of War and another of the legendary three.

2 - Zhuge Liang, or Kongming, was a Chinese military strategist and inventor during the Three Kingdoms period. His reputation only grew when he lived in seclusion, earning him the nickname "Crouching Dragon" or "Hidden Dragon."

Originally published in Chinese in *Science Fiction World,* 2015, issue 10.

Translated and published in partnership with Storycom.

ABOUT THE AUTHOR

Luo Longxiang was born in 1981, deep in the mountains of Guangxi province on the China's southern border, where he studied Chemical Engineering at Guangxi University. After publishing his first sci-fi story in 2003, his fans began to refer to the mysterious author as "Master Luo," in reference to his hermit-like existence far away from the crowded cities of the coast and northern plains. Of the eleven stories he was written over the past decade, six have earned a Milky Way Award. His works are known for their massive scope, dealing almost exclusively with the question of humanity's eventual survival in space. Since 2007, he has been working to complete the Planetship Alliance series—an epic space opera recounting the tragic history of mankind's colonization of the universe.

The Mighty Slinger

KAREN LORD AND TOBIAS S. BUCKELL

Earth began to rise over the lunar hills as the Mighty Slinger and the Rovers readied the Tycho stage for their performance. Tapping his microphone, Euclid noticed that Kumi barely glanced at the sight as he set up his djembe and pan assembly, but Jeni froze and stared up at the blue disk, her bass still limp between her hands.

"It's not going anywhere," Kumi muttered. His long, graying dreadlocks swayed gently in the heavy gravity of the moon and tapped the side of a pan with a muted "ting."

"It'll be there after the concert . . . and after our trip, *and* after we revive from our next long-sleep."

"Let her look," Vega admonished. "You should always stop for beauty. It vanishes too soon."

"She taking too long to set up," Kumi said. "You-all call her Zippy but she ain't zippy at all."

Euclid chuckled as Jeni shot a stink look at her elder and mentor. She whipped the bass out stiff like she meant business. Her fingers gripped and danced on the narrow surface in a quick, defiant riff.

Raising his mic-wand at the back, Vega captured the sound as it bounced back from the lunar dome performance area. He fed the echo through the house speakers, ending it with a punctuating note of Kumi's locks hitting the pan with a ting and Euclid's laughter rumbling quietly in the background. Dhaka, the last of the Rovers, came in live with a cheerful fanfare on her patented Delirium, an instrument that looked like a harmonium had had a painful collision with a large quantity of alloy piping.

An asteroid-thin man in a black suit slipped past the velvet ropes marking off the VIP section and nodded at Euclid. "Yes sir. Your pay's been deposited, the spa is booked, and your places in the long-sleep pool are reserved."

“Did you add the depreciation-protection insurance this time?” Euclid answered, his voice cold with bitter memory. “If your grandfather had sense I could be retired by now.”

Kumi looked sharply over. The man in the suit shifted about. “Of course I’ll add the insurance,” he mumbled.

“Thank you, Mr. Jones,” Euclid said, in a tone that was not at all thankful.

“There’s, ah, someone else who would like to talk to you,” the event coordinator said.

“Not now Jones.” Euclid turned away to face his band. “Only forty minutes to curtain time and we need to focus.”

“It’s about Earth,” Jones said.

Euclid turned back. “That rumor?”

Jones shook his head. “Not a rumor. Not even a joke. The Rt Hon. Patience Bouscholte got notification this morning. She wants to talk to you.”

The Rt Hon. Patience Bouscholte awaited him in one of the skyboxes poised high over the rim of the crater. Before it: the stands that would soon be filling up, slanting along the slope that created a natural amphitheater to the stage. Behind it: the gray hills and rocky wasteland of the Moon.

“Mr. Slinger!” she said. Her tightly wound hair and brown spidersilk head scarf bobbed in a slightly delayed reaction to the lunar gravity. “A pleasure to finally meet you. I’m a huge admirer of your sound.”

He sat down, propped his snakeskin magnet-boots up against the chairback in front of him, and gave her a cautious look. “Madame Minister. To what do I owe the pleasure?”

All of the band were members of the Rock Devils Cohort and Consociate Fusion, almost a million strong, all contract workers in the asteroid belt. They were all synced up on the same long-sleep schedule as their cohort, whether working the rock or touring as a band. And here was a Minister from the RDCCF’s Assembly asking to speak with him.

The RDCCF wasn’t a country. It was just one of many organizations for people who worked in space because there was nothing left for them on Earth. But to Euclid, meeting the Rt Hon. Patience Bouscholte felt like meeting a Member of Parliament from the old days. Euclid was slightly intimidated, but he wasn’t going to show it. He put an arm casually over the empty seat beside him.

“They said you were far quieter in person than on stage. They were right.” Bouscholte held up a single finger before he could reply, and pointed to two women in all-black bulletproof suits who were busy scanning the room with small wands. They gave a thumbs up as Bouscholte cocked her head in their direction, and retreated to stand on either side of the entrance.

She turned back to Euclid. "Tell me, Mr. Slinger, how much have you heard about the Solar Development Charter and their plans for Earth?"

So it was true? He leaned toward her. "Why would they have any plans for Earth? I've heard they're stretched thin enough building the Glitter Ring."

"They are. They're stretched more than thin. They're functionally bankrupt. So the SDC is taking up a new tranche of preferred shares for a secondary redevelopment scheme. They want to 'redevelop' Earth, and that will *not* be to our benefit."

"Well then." Euclid folded his arms and leaned back. "And you thought you'd tell an old calypso singer that because . . . ?"

"Because I need your rhymes, Mr. Slinger."

Euclid had done that before, in the days before his last long-sleep, when fame was high and money had not yet evaporated. Dishing out juicy new gossip to help Assembly contract negotiations. Leaking information to warn the workers all across the asteroid belt. Hardworking miners on contract, struggling to survive the long nights and longer sleeps. Sing them a song about how the SDC was planning to screw them over again. He knew that gig well.

He had thought that was why he'd been brought to see her, to get a little something to add extempo to a song tonight. Get the Belt all riled up. But if this was about Earth . . . ? Earth was a garbage dump. Humanity had sucked it dry like a vampire and left its husk to spiral toward death as people moved outward to bigger and better things.

"I don't sing about Earth anymore. The cohorts don't pay attention to the old stuff. Why should they care? It's not going anywhere."

Then she told him. Explained that the SDC was going to beautify Earth. Re-terraform it. Make it into a new garden of Eden for the rich and idle of Mars and Venus.

"How?" he asked, skeptical.

"Scorched Earth. They're going to bomb the mother planet with comets. Full demolition. The last of us shipped into the Ring to form new cohorts, new generations of indentured servitude. A clean slate to redesign their brave new world. That is what I mean when I say *not to our benefit*."

He exhaled slowly. "You think a few little lyrics can change any of that?" The wealth of Venus, Mars, and Jupiter dwarfed the cohorts in their hollowed out, empty old asteroids.

"One small course adjustment at the start can change an entire orbit by the end of a journey," she said.

"So you want me to harass the big people up in power for you, now?"

Bouscholte shook her head. "We need you to be our emissary. We, the Assembly, the last representatives of the drowned lands and the dying islands, are calling upon you. Are you with us or not?"

Euclid thought back to the days of breezes and mango trees. "And if they don't listen to us?"

Bouscholte leaned in close and touched his arm. "The majority of our cohort are indentured to the Solar Development Charter until the Glitter Ring is complete. But, Mr. Slinger, answer me this: where do you think that leaves us after we finish the Ring, the largest project humanity has ever attempted?"

Euclid knew. After the asteroid belt had been transformed into its new incarnation, a sun-girdling, sun-powered device for humanity's next great leap, it would no longer be home.

There were few resources left in the Belt; the big planets had got there first and mined it all. Euclid had always known the hollow shells that had been left behind. The work on the Glitter Ring. The long-sleep so that they didn't exhaust resources as they waited for pieces of the puzzle to slowly float from place to appointed place.

Bouscholte continued. "If we can't go back to Earth, they'll send us further out. Our cohorts will end up scattered to the cold, distant areas of the system, out to the Oort Cloud. And we'll live long enough to see that."

"You think you can stop that?"

"Maybe, Mr. Slinger. There is almost nothing we can broadcast that the big planets can't listen to. When we go into long-sleep they can hack our communications, but they can't keep us from talking, and they'll never stop our songs."

"It's a good dream," Euclid said softly, for the first time in the conversation looking up at the view over the skybox. He'd avoided looking at it. To Jeni it was a beautiful blue dot, but for Euclid all it did was remind him of what he'd lost. "But they won't listen."

"You must understand, you are just one piece in a much bigger game. Our people are in place, not just in the cohorts, but everywhere, all throughout the system. They'll listen to your music and make the right moves at the right time. The SDC can't move to destroy and rebuild Earth until the Glitter Ring is finished, but when it's finished they'll find they have underestimated us—as long as we coordinate in a way that no one suspects."

"Using songs? Nah. Impossible," he declared bluntly.

She shook her head, remarkably confident. "All you have to do is be the messenger. We'll handle the tactics. You forget who you're speaking to. The Bouscholte family tradition has always been about the long game. Who was my father? What positions do my sons hold, my granddaughters? Euclid Slinger . . . Babatunde . . . listen to me. How do you think an aging calypso star gets booked to do an expensive, multi-planetary tour to the capitals of the Solar System, the seats of power? By chance?"

She called him that name as if she were his friend, his inner-circle intimate. Kumi named him that years . . . decades ago. *Too wise for your years. You were here before*, he'd said. *The Father returns, sent back for a reason.* Was this the reason?

"I accept the mission," he said.

Day. Me say Day-Oh. Earthrise come and me want go . . .

Euclid looked up, smiled. Let the chord go. He wouldn't be so blatant as to wink at the VIP section, but he knew that there was a fellow Rock Devil out there, listening out for certain songs and recording Vega's carefully assembled samples to strip for data and instructions in a safe location. Vega knew, of course. Had to, in order to put together the info packets. Dhaka knew a little but had begged not to know more, afraid she might say the wrong thing to the wrong person. Jeni was still, after her first long-sleep, nineteen in body and mind, so no, she did not know, and anyway how could he tell her when he was still dragging his feet on telling Kumi?

And there was Kumi, frowning at him after the end of the concert as they sprawled in the green room, taking a quick drink before the final packing up. "Baba, you on this nostalgia kick for real."

"You don't like it?" Euclid teased him. "All that sweet, sweet soca you grew up studying, all those kaiso legends you try to emulate?"

"That ain't your sound, man."

Euclid shrugged. "We can talk about that next time we're in the studio. Now we got a party to be at!"

After twenty-five years of long-sleep, Euclid thought Mars looked much the same, except maybe a little greener, a little wetter. Perhaps that was why the directors of the SDC-MME had chosen to host their bash in a gleaming biodome that overlooked a charming little lake. Indoor foliage matched to outer landscape in a lush canopy and artificial lights hovered in competition with the stars and satellites beyond.

"Damn show-offs," Dhaka muttered. "Am I supposed to be impressed?"

"*I* am," Jeni said shamelessly, selecting a stimulant cocktail from an offered tray. Kumi smoothly took it from her and replaced it with another, milder option. She looked outraged.

"Keep a clear head, Zippy," Vega said quietly. "We're not among friends."

That startled her out of her anger. Kumi looked a little puzzled himself, but he accepted Vega's support without challenge.

Euclid listened with half his attention. He had just noticed an opportunity. "Kumi, all of you, come with me. Let's greet the CEO and offer our thanks for this lovely party."

Kumi came to his side. "What's going on?"

Euclid lowered his voice. "Come, listen and find out."

The CEO acknowledged them as they approached, but Euclid could sense from the body language that the busy executive would give them as much time as dictated by courtesy and not a bit more. No matter that Euclid was a credentialed ambassador for the RDCCF, authorized by the Assembly. He could already tell how this meeting would go.

"Thank you for hosting us, Mx. Ashe," Euclid said, donning a pleasant, grinning mask. "It's always a pleasure to kick off a tour at the Mars Mining and Energy Megaplex."

"Thank *you*," the executive replied. "Your music is very popular with our hands."

"Pardon?" Kumi enquired, looking in confusion at the executive's fingers wrapped around an ornate cocktail glass.

"Our employees in the asteroid belt."

Kumi looked unamused. Euclid moved on quickly. "Yes. You merged with the SDC . . . pardon me, we are still trying to catch up on twenty-five years of news . . . about ten years ago?"

A little pride leaked past the politeness. "Buyout, not merger. Only the name has survived, to maintain continuity and branding."

Euclid saw Dhaka smirk and glance at Vega, who looked a little sour. He was still slightly bitter that his ex-husband had taken everything in the divorce except for the de la Vega surname, the name under which he had become famous and which Vega was forced to keep for the sake of convenience.

"But don't worry," the CEO continued. "The Glitter Ring was always conceptualized as a project that would be measured in generations. Corporations may rise and fall, but the work will go on. Everything remains on schedule and all the hands . . . all the—how do you say—*cohorts* are in no danger of losing their jobs."

"So, the cohorts can return to Earth after the Ring is completed?" Euclid asked directly.

Mx. Ashe took a careful sip of bright purple liquid before replying. "I did not say that."

"But I thought the Earth development project was set up to get the SDC a secondary round of financing, to solve their financial situation," Dhaka demanded, her brow creasing. "You've bought them out, so is that still necessary?"

Mx. Ashe nodded calmly. "True, but we have a more complex vision for the Glitter Ring than the SDC envisioned, and so funding must be vastly increased. Besides, taking money for a planned redevelopment of Earth and then not doing it would, technically, be fraud. The SDC-MME will follow through. I won't bore you with the details, but our expertise on geo-engineering is unparalleled."

"You've been dropping comets on vast, uninhabited surfaces," Dhaka said. "I understand the theory, but Earth isn't Venus or Mars. There's thousands of years of history and archeology. And there are still people living there. How are you going to move a billion people?"

Mx. Ashe looked coldly at Dhaka. "We're still in the middle of building a Ring around the sun, Mx. Miriam. I'm sure my successors on the Board will have it all figured out by the next time we wake you up. We understand the concerns raised, but after all, people have invested trillions in this project. Our lawyers are in the process of responding to all requests and lawsuits, and we will stand by the final ruling of the courts."

Euclid spoke quickly, blunt in his desperation. "Can't you reconsider, find another project to invest in? Earth's a mess, we all know it, but we always thought we'd have something to come back to."

"I'm sure a man of your means could afford a plot on New Earth—" Mx. Ashe began.

"I've seen the pricing," Vega cut in dryly. "Musicians don't make as much as you think."

"What about the cohorts?" Jeni said sadly. "No one in the cohorts will be able to afford to go back."

Mx. Ashe stepped back from the verbal bombardment. "This is all speculation. The cohorts are still under contract to work on the Glitter Ring. Once they have finished, negotiations about their relocation can begin. Now, if you will excuse me, have a good night and enjoy the party!"

Euclid watched despondently as the CEO walked away briskly. The Rovers stood silently around him, their faces somber. Kumi was the first to speak. "*Now* I understand the nostalgia kick."

*The SDC, now with the MMEYou and I both knowThey don't stand for you and me*There was still a tour to play. The band moved from Elysium

City to Electris Station, then Achillis Fons, where they played in front of the Viking Museum.

The long-sleep on the way to Mars had been twenty-five years. Twenty-five years off, one year on. That was the shift the Rock Devils Cohort and Consociation Fusion had agreed to, the key clause in the contract Euclid had signed way-back-when in an office built into the old New York City seawall.

That gave them a whole year on Mars. Mx. Ashe may have shut them down, but Euclid wasn't done yet. Not by a long shot.

Kumi started fretting barely a month in.

"Jeni stepping out with one of the VIPs," he told Euclid.

"She's nineteen. What you expecting? A celibate band member? I don't see you ignoring anyone coming around when we breaking down."

Kumi shook his head. "No Baba, that's one thing. This is the same one she's seeing. Over and over. Since we arrived here. She's sticky sweet on him."

"Kumi, we got bigger things to worry about."

"Earth, I know. Man, look, I see why you're upset." Kumi grabbed his hand. "I miss it too. But we getting old, Baba. I just pass sixty. How much longer I could do this? Maybe we focus on the tour and invest the money so that we can afford to go back some day."

"I can't give it up that easy," Euclid said to his oldest friend. "We going to have troubles?"

Back when Euclid was working the rocks, Kumi had taken him under his wing. Taught him how to sing the old songs while they moved their one-person pods into position to drill them out. Then they'd started singing at the start of shifts and soon that took off into a full career. They'd traveled all through the Belt, from big old Ceres to the tiniest cramped mining camps.

Kumi sucked his teeth. "That first time you went extempo back on Pallas, you went after that foreman who'd been skimping on airlock maintenance? You remember?"

Euclid laughed. "I was angry. The airlock blew out and I wet myself waiting for someone to come pick me up."

"When you started singing different lyrics, making them up on the spot, I didn't follow you at first. But you got the SDC to fire him when the video went viral. That's why I called you Baba. So, no, you sing and I'll find my way around your words. Always. But let me ask you—think about what Ashe said. You really believe this fight's worth it?"

Euclid bit his lip.

"We have concerts to give in the Belt and Venus yet," he told Kumi. "We're not done yet."

Five months in, the Martians began to turn. The concerts had been billed as cross-cultural events, paid for by the Pan-Human Solar Division of Cultural Affairs and the Martian University's division of Inter-Human Musicology Studies school.

Euclid, on stage, hadn't noticed at first. He'd been trying to find another way to match up MME with "screw me" and some lyrics in between. Then a comparison to Mars and its power, and the people left behind on Earth.

But he noticed when *this* crowd turned.

Euclid had grown used to the people of the big planets just sitting and listening to his music. No one was moving about. No hands in the air. Even if you begged them, they weren't throwing their hands out. No working, no grinding, no nothing. They sat in seats and *appreciated.*

He didn't remember when they turned. He would see it on video later. Maybe it was when he called out the "rape" of Earth with the "red tape" of the SDC-MME and made a visual of "red" Mars that tied to the "red" tape, but suddenly those chair-sitting intercultural appreciators stood up.

And it wasn't to jump.

The crowd started shouting back. The sound cut out. Security and the venue operators swept in and moved them off the stage.

Back in the green room, Jeni rounded on Euclid. "What the hell was that?" she shouted.

"Extempo," Euclid said simply.

Kumi tried to step between them. "Zippy—"

"No!" She pushed him aside. Dhaka, in the corner of the room, started disassembling the Delirium, carefully putting the pieces away in a g-force protected aerogel case, carefully staying out of the brewing fight. Vega folded his arms and stood to a side, watching. "I damn well know what extempo is. I'm young, not ignorant."

Everyone was tired. The heavy gravity, the months of touring already behind them. "This always happens. A fight always come halfway through," Euclid said. "Talk to me."

"You're doing extempo like you're in a small free concert in the Belt, on a small rock. But this isn't going after some corrupt contractor," Jeni snapped. "You're calling out a whole planet now? All Martians? You crazy?"

"One person or many, you think I shouldn't?"

Euclid understood. Jeni had been working pods like he had at the same age. Long, grueling shifts spent in a tiny bubble of plastic where you rebreathed your own stench so often you forgot what clean air tasted like. Getting into the band had been her way "off the rock." This was her big gamble out of tedium. His too, back in the day.

"You're not entertaining people. You're pissing them off," she said.

Euclid sucked his teeth. "Calypso been vexing people since all the way back. And never mind calypso, Zippy, entertainment isn't just escape. Artists always talking back, always insolent."

"They paid us and flew us across the solar system to sing the song they wanted. Sing the fucking song for them the way they want. Even just the Banana Boat Song you're messing with and going extempo. That shit's carved in stone, Euclid. Sing the damn lyrics."

Euclid looked at her like she'd lost her mind. "That song was *never* for them. Problem is it get sung too much and you abstract it and then everyone forget that song is a blasted lament. Well, let me educate you, Ms Baptiste. The Banana Boat Song is a mournful song about people getting their backs broken hard in labor and still using call and response to help the community sync up, dig deep, and find the power to work harder 'cause *dem ain't had no choice*."

He stopped. A hush fell in the green room.

Euclid continued. "It's not a 'smile and dance for them' song. The big planets don't own that song. It was never theirs. It was never carved in stone. I'll make it ours for *here*, for *now*, and I'll go extempo. I'm not done. Zippy, I'm just getting started."

She nodded. "Then I'm gone."

Just like that, she spun around and grabbed her bass.

Kumi glared at Euclid. "I promised her father I'd keep an eye on her—"

"Go," Euclid said calmly, but he was suddenly scared that his oldest friend, the pillar of his little band, would walk out the green room door with the newest member and never come back.

Kumi came back an hour later. He looked suddenly old . . . those raw-sun wrinkles around his eyes, the stooped back. But it wasn't just gravity pulling him down. "She's staying on Mars."

Euclid turned to the door. "Let me go speak to her. I'm the one she angry with."

"No." Kumi put a hand on his shoulder. "That wasn't just about you. She staying with someone. She's not just leaving the band, she leaving the cohort. Got a VIP, a future, someone she thinks she'll build a life with."

She was gone. Like that.

Vega still had her riffs, though. He grumbled about the extra work, but he could weave the recorded samples in and out of the live music.

Kumi got an invitation to the wedding. It took place the week before the Rovers left Mars for the big tour of the asteroid belt.

Euclid wasn't invited.

He did a small, open concert for the Rock Devils working on Deimos. It was just him and Vega and fifty miners in one of the teardown areas of the tiny moon. Euclid sang for them just as pointedly as ever.

*So it's up to us, you and meto put an end to this catastrophe.Them ain't got neither conscience nor heart.We got to pitch in and do our part'cause if this Earth demolition beginwe won't even have a part/pot to pitch/piss in.*Touring in the Belt always gave him a strange feeling of mingled nostalgia and dissonance. There were face-to-face reunions and continued correspondence with friends and relatives of their cohort, who shared the same times of waking and long-sleep, spoke the same language, and remembered the same things. But there were also administrators and officials, who kept their own schedule, and workers from cohorts on a different frequency—all strangers from a forgotten distant past or an unknown near-present. Only the most social types kept up-to-date on everything, acting as temporal diplomats, translating jokes and explaining new tech and jargon to smooth communication between groups.

Ziamara Bouscholte was social. Very social. Euclid had seen plenty of that frivolous-idle behavior from political families and nouveau-nobility like the family Jeni had married into, but given *that* surname and the fact that she had been assigned as their tour liaison, he recognized very quickly that she was a spy.

"Big tours in the Belt are boredom and chaos," he warned her, thinking about the argument with Jeni. "Lots of downtime slinging from asteroid to asteroid punctuated by concert mayhem when we arrive."

She grinned. "Don't worry about me. I know exactly how to deal with boredom and chaos."

She didn't lie. She was all-business on board, briefing Vega on the latest cryptography and answering Dhaka's questions about the technological advances that were being implemented in Glitter Ring construction. Then the butterfly emerged for the concerts and parties as she wrangled fans and dignitaries with a smiling enthusiasm that never flagged.

The Vesta concert was their first major stop. The Mighty Slinger and his Rovers peeked out from the wings of the stage and watched the local opening act finishing up their last set.

Kumi brought up something that had been nagging Euclid for a while. "Baba, you notice how small the crowds are? *This* is our territory, not Mars. Last big tour we had to broadcast over Vesta because everything was sold out."

Vega agreed. "Look at this audience. Thin. I could excuse the other venues for size, but not this one."

"I know why," Dhaka said. "I can't reach half my friends who agreed to meet up. All I'm getting from them are long-sleep off-shift notices."

"I thought it was just me," Kumi said. "Did SDC-MME leave cohorts in long-sleep? Cutting back on labor?"

Dhaka nodded. "Zia mentioned some changes in the project schedule. You know the Charter's not going to waste money feeding us if we're not working."

Euclid felt a surge of anger. "We'll be out of sync when they wake up again. That messes up the whole cohort. You sure they're doing this to cut labor costs, or to weaken us as a collective?"

Dhaka shrugged. "I don't like it one bit, but I don't know if it's out of incompetence or malice."

"Time to go," said Vega, his eyes on the openers as they exited stage left.

The Rovers drifted on stage and started freestyling, layering sound on sound. Euclid waited until they were all settled in and jamming hard before running out and snagging his mic. He was still angry, and the adrenaline amped up his performance as he commandeered the stage to rant about friends and lovers lost for a whole year to long-sleep.

Then he heard something impossible: Kumi stumbled on the beat. Euclid looked back at the Rovers to see Vega frozen. A variation of one of Jeni's famous riffs was playing, but Vega shook his head *not me* to Dhaka's confused sideways glance.

Zia's voice came on the sound system, booming over the music. "Rock Devils cohort, we have a treat for you! On stage for the first time in twenty-five years, please welcome Rover bassist Jeni 'Zippy' Baptiste!"

Jeni swooped in from the wings with another stylish riff, bounced off one of the decorated pylons, then flew straight to Kumi and wrapped him in a tumbling hug, bass and all. Prolonged cheering from the crowd drowned out the music. Euclid didn't know whether to be furious or overjoyed at Zia for springing the surprise on them in public. Vega smoothly covered for the absent percussion and silent bass while Dhaka went wild on the Delirium. It was a horrible place for a reunion, but they'd take it. Stage lighting made it hard to tell, but Jeni did look older and . . . stronger? More sure of herself?

Euclid floated over to her at the end of the song as the applause continued to crash over them all. "Welcome back, Zippy," he said. "You're still good—better, even."

Her laugh was full and sincere. "I've been listening to our recordings for twenty-five years, playing along with you every day while you were in long-sleep. Of course I'm better."

"You missed us," he stated proudly.

"I did." She swatted a tear out of the air between them with the back of her hand. "I missed *this*. Touring for our cohort. Riling up the powers that be."

He raised his eyebrows. "*Now* you want to shake things up? What changed?"

She shook her head sadly. "Twenty-five years, Baba. I have a daughter, now. She's twenty, training as an engineer on Mars. She's going to join the cohort when she's finished and I want more for her. I want a future for her."

He hugged her tight while the crowd roared in approval. "Get back on that bass," he whispered. "We got a show to finish!"

He didn't bother to ask if the nouveau-nobility husband had approved of the rebel Rover Jeni. He suspected not.

In the green room Jeni wrapped her legs around a chair and hung a glass of beer in the air next to her.

"Used to be it would fall slowly down to the floor," Jeni said, pointing at her drink. "They stripped most of Vesta's mass for the Ring. It's barely a shell here."

Dhaka shoved a foot in a wall strap and settled in perpendicular to Jeni. She swirled the whiskey glass around in the air. Despite the glass being designed for zero gravity, her practiced flip of the wrist tossed several globules free that very slowly wobbled their way through the air toward her. "We're passing into final stage preparations for the Ring. SDC-MME is panicking a bit because the projections for energy and the initial test results don't match. And the computers are having trouble managing stable orbits."

The Glitter Ring was a Dyson Ring, a necklace of solar power stations and sails built around the sun to capture a vast percentage of its energy. The power needs of the big planets had begun to outstrip the large planetary solar and mirror arrays a hundred years ago. Overflight and shadow rights for solar gathering stations had started turning into a series of low-grade orbital economic wars. The Charter had been created to handle the problem system-wide.

Build a ring of solar power catchments in orbit around the sun at a slight angle to the plane of the solar system. No current solar rights would be abridged, but it could catapult humanity into a new industrial era. A great leap forward. Unlimited, unabridged power.

But if it didn't work . . .

Dhaka nodded at all the serious faces. "Don't look so glum. The cohort programmers are working on flocking algorithms to try and simplify how the solar stations keep in orbit. Follow some simple rules about what's around you and let complex emergent orbits develop."

"I'm more worried about the differences in output," Jeni muttered. "While you've been in long-sleep they've been developing orbital stations out past Jupiter with the assumption that there would be beamed power to follow. They're building mega-orbitals throughout the system on the assumption that the Ring's going to work. They've even started moving people off Earth into temporary housing in orbit."

"Temporary?" Euclid asked from across the room, interrupting before Dhaka and Jeni got deep into numbers and words like exajoules, quantum efficiency, price per watt, and all the other boring crap. He'd cared intimately about that when he first joined the cohort. Now, not so much.

"We're talking bubble habitats with thinner shells than Vesta right now. They use a layer of water for radiation shielding, but they lack resources and they're not well balanced. These orbitals have about a couple hundred thousand people each, and they're rated to last fifty to sixty years." Jeni shook her head, and Euclid was forced to stop seeing the nineteen-year-old Zippy and recognize the concerned forty-four year old she'd become. "They're risking a lot."

"Why would anyone agree?" Vega asked. "It sounds like suicide."

"It's gotten worse on Earth. Far worse. Everyone is just expecting to hit the reset button after the Glitter Ring goes online. Everyone's holding their breath."

Dhaka spoke up. "Okay, enough cohort bullshit. Let's talk about you. The band's heading back to long-sleep soon—and then what, Zippy? You heading back to Mars and your daughter?"

Jeni looked around the room hesitantly. "Lara's never been to Venus, and I promised her she could visit me . . . if you'll have me?"

"If?" Vega laughed. "I hated playing those recordings of you. Rather hear it live."

"I'm not as zippy up and down the chords as I used to be, you know," Jeni warned. Everyone was turning to look at Euclid.

"It's a more confident sound," he said with a smile. Dhaka whipped globules of whiskey at them and laughed.

Kumi beamed, no doubt already dreaming about meeting his "granddaughter."

"Hey, Zippy," Euclid said. "Here's to change. *Good* change."

"Maybe," she smiled and slapped his raised hand in agreement and approval. "Let's dream on that."

The first few days after long-sleep were never pleasant, but this awakening was the worst of Euclid's experience. He slowly remembered who he was, and how to speak, and the names of the people who sat quietly with him in the lounge after their sessions with the medics. For a while they silently watched the high cities of Venus glinting in the clouds below their orbit from viewports near the long-sleep pools.

Later they began to ask questions, later they realized that something was very wrong. They'd been asleep for fifty years. Two long-sleeps, not the usual single sleep.

"Everyone gone silent back on Vesta," Dhaka said.

"Did we get idled?" Euclid demanded. They were a band, not workers. They shouldn't have been idled.

The medics didn't answer their questions. They continued to deflect everything until one morning an officer turned up, dressed in black sub-uniform with empty holster belt, as if he had left his weapons and armor just outside the door. He looked barely twenty, far too young for the captain's insignia on his shoulders.

He spoke with slow, stilted formality. "Mr. Slinger, Mr. Djansi, Mr. de la Vega, Ms Miriam, and Ms Baptiste—thank you for your patience. I'm Captain Abrams. We're sorry for the delay, but your recovery was complicated."

"Complicated!" Kumi looked disgusted. "Can you explain why we had two long-sleeps instead of one? Fifty years? We had a contract!"

"And *we* had a war." The reply was unexpectedly sharp. "Be glad you missed it."

"Our first interplanetary war? That's not the change I wanted," Euclid muttered to Vega.

"What happened?" Jeni asked, her voice barely a whisper. "My daughter, she's on Mars, is she safe?"

The officer glanced away in a momentary flash of vulnerability and guilt. "You have two weeks for news and correspondence with your cohort and others. We can provide political summaries and psychological care for your readjustment. After that, your tour begins. Transport down to the cities has been arranged. I just . . . I have to say . . . we still need you now, more than ever."

"The *rass*?" Kumi stared at the soldier, spreading his arms.

Again that touch of vulnerability as the young soldier replied with a slight stammer. "Please. We need you. You're legends to the entire system now, not just the cohorts."

"The hell does that mean?" Vega asked as the boy-captain left.

Jeni's daughter had managed one long-sleep but woke on schedule while they stayed in storage. The war was over by then, but Martian infrastructure had been badly damaged and skilled workers were needed for longer than the standard year or two. Lara had died after six years of "extra time," casualty of a radiation exposure accident on Deimos.

They gathered around Jeni when she collapsed to her knees and wept, grieving for the child they had never known.

Their correspondence was scattered across the years, their cohort truly broken as it had been forced to take cover, retreat, or fight. The war had started in Earth orbit after a temporary habitat split apart, disgorging water, air, and people into vacuum. Driven by desperation and fury, several other orbital inhabitants had launched an attack on SDC-MME-owned stations, seeking a secure environment to live, and revenge for their dead.

Conflict became widespread and complicated. The orbital habitats were either negotiating for refugees, building new orbitals, or fighting for the SDC-MME. Mars got involved when the government sent its military to protect the Martian investment in the SDC-MME. Jupiter, which was now its own functioning techno-demarchy, had struck directly at the Belt, taking over a large portion of the Glitter Ring.

Millions had died as rocks were flung between the worlds, and ships danced around each other in the vacuum. People fought hand-to-hand in civil wars inside hollowed out asteroids, gleaming metal orbitals, and in the cold silence of space.

Humanity had carried war out of Earth and into the great beyond.

Despite the grim history lesson, as the band shared notes and checked their financial records, one thing became clear. They *were* legends. The music of the Mighty Slinger and the Rovers had become the sound of the war generation and beyond: a common bond that the cohorts could still claim, and battle hymns for the Earth emigrants who had launched out from their decayed temporary orbitals. Anti-SDC-MME songs became treasured anthems. The Rovers' songs sold billions, the *covers* of their songs sold billions. There were tribute bands and spin-off bands and a fleet of touring bands. They had spawned an entire subgenre of music.

"We're rich at last," Kumi said ruefully. "I thought I'd enjoy it more."

Earth was still there, still a mess, but Vega found hope in news from his kin. For decades, Pacific Islanders had stubbornly roved over their drowned states in vast fleets, refusing resettlement to the crowded cities and tainted badlands of the continents. In the last fifty years, their floating harbors had evolved from experimental platforms to self-sustaining cities. For them, the war had been nothing but a few nights filled with shooting stars and the occasional planetfall of debris.

The Moon and Venus had fared better in the war than Mars, but the real shock was the Ring. According to Dhaka, the leap in progress was marked, even for fifty years. Large sections were now fully functional and had been used during the war for refueling, surveillance, barracks, and prisons.

"Unfortunately, that means that the purpose of the Ring has drifted once again," she warned. "The military adapted it to their purposes, and returning it to civilian use will take some time."

"But what about the Assembly?" Euclid asked her one day when they were in the studio, shielded from surveillance by noise and interference from Vega's crafting. "Do they still care about the purpose of the Ring? Do you think we still have a mission?"

The war had ended without a clear victor. The SDC-MME had collapsed and the board had been tried, convicted and exiled to long-sleep until a clear treaty could be hammered out. Jupiter, Mars, Venus, and some of the richer orbitals had assumed the shares and responsibility of the original solar charter. A tenuous peace existed.

Dhaka nodded. "I was wondering that too, but look, here's the name of the company that's organizing our tour."

Euclid leaned in to read her screen. *Bouscholte, Bouscholte & Abrams.*

Captain Abrams revealed nothing until they were all cramped into the tiny cockpit of a descent craft for Venus' upper atmosphere.

He checked for listening devices with a tiny wand, and then, satisfied, faced them all. "The Bouscholte family would like to thank you for your service. We want you to understand that you are in an even better position to help us, and we need that help now, more than ever."

They'd come this far. Euclid looked around at the Rovers. They all leaned in closer.

"The Director of Consolidated Ring Operations and Planetary Reconstruction will be at your concert tonight." Abrams handed Euclid a small chip. "You will give this to him—personally. It's a quantum encrypted key that only Director Cutler can access."

"What's in it?" Dhaka asked.

Abrams looked out the window. They were about to fall into the yellow and green clouds. The green was something to do with floating algae engineered for the planet, step one of the eventual greening of Venus. "Something Cutler won't like. Or maybe a bribe. I don't know. But it's an encouragement for the Director to consider a proposal."

"Can you tell us what the proposal is?"

"Yes." Abrams looked at the band. "Either stop the redevelopment of Earth and further cement the peace by returning the orbitals inhabitants to the surface, or . . . "

Everyone waited as Abrams paused dramatically.

" . . . approve a cargo transit across Mercury's inner orbit to the far side of the Glitter Ring, and give us the contracts for rebuilding the orbital habitats."

Dhaka frowned. "I wasn't expecting something so boring after the big 'or' there, Captain."

Abrams smiled. "One small course adjustment at the start can change an entire orbit by the end of a journey," he said to Euclid.

That sounded familiar.

"Either one of those is important?" Euclid asked. "But you won't say why."

"Not even in this little cabin. I'm sure I got the bugs, but in case I didn't." Abrams shrugged. "Here we are. Ready to change the solar system, Mr. Slinger?"

Venusian cities were more impressive when viewed from the outside. Vast, silvery spheres clustered thickly in the upper atmosphere, trailing tethers and tubes to the surface like a dense herd of giant cephalopods. Inside, the decor was sober, spare and disappointing, hinting at a slow postwar recovery.

The band played their first concert in a half-century to a frighteningly respectful and very exclusive audience of the rich and powerful. Then it was off to a reception where they awkwardly sipped imported wine and smiled as their assigned liaison, a woman called Halford, briskly introduced and dismissed awestruck fans for seconds of small talk and a quick snap.

"And this is Petyr Cutler," Halford announced. "Director of Consolidated Ring Operations and Planetary Reconstruction."

Bodyguards quickly made a wall, shepherding the Director in for his moment.

Cutler was a short man with loose, sandy hair and bit of orbital sunburn. "So pleased to meet you," he said. "Call me Petyr."

He came in for the vigorous handshake, and Euclid had already palmed the small chip. He saw Abrams on the periphery of the crowd, watching. Nodded.

Cutler's already reddened cheeks flushed as he looked down at the chip. "Is that—"

"Yes." Euclid locked eyes with him. The Director. One of the most powerful people in the entire solar system.

Cutler broke the gaze and looked down at his feet. "You can't blackmail me, not even with this. I can't change policy."

"So you still redeveloping Earth?" Euclid asked, his tone already dull with resignation.

"I've been around before you were born, Mr. Slinger. I know how generational projects go. They build their own momentum. No one wants to become the executive who shut down two hundred years of progress, who couldn't see it through to the end. Besides, wars aren't cheap. We have to repay our citizens who invested in war bonds, the corporations that gave us tech on credit. The Earth Reconstruction project is the only thing that can give us the funds to stay afloat."

Somehow, his words eased the growing tightness in Euclid's chest. "I'm supposed to ask you something else, then."

Cutler looked suspicious. He also looked around at his bodyguards, wanting to leave. "Your people have big asks, Mr. Slinger."

"This is smaller. We need your permission to move parts across Mercury's orbit, close to the sun, but your company has been denying that request. The Rock Devils cohort also wants to rebuild the surviving temporary Earth orbitals."

"Post-war security measures are still in place—"

"Security measures my ass." Jeni spoke so loudly, so intensely that the whole room went quiet to hear her.

"Jeni—" Kumi started.

"No. We've sacrificed our lives and our children's lives for your damn Ring. We've made it our entire reason for existence and we're tired. One last section to finish, that could finish in less than three decades if you let us take that shortcut to get the last damn parts in place and let us go work on something worthwhile. We're tired. Finish the blasted project and let us live."

Kumi stood beside her and put his arm around her shoulders. She leaned into him, but she did not falter. Her gaze stayed hard and steady on the embarrassed Director who was now the center of a room of shocked, sympathetic, judging looks.

"We need clearance from Venus," Director Cutler mumbled.

Euclid started humming a quick back beat. Cutler looked startled. "*Director*," Euclid sang, voice low. He reached for the next word the sentence needed to bridge. *Dictator*. How to string that in with . . . something to do with the project finishing *later*.

He'd been on the stage singing the old lyrics people wanted to hear. His songs that had once been extempo, but now were carved in stone by a new generation.

But right here, with the bodyguards all around them, Euclid wove a quick song damning him for preventing progress in the solar system and making trouble for the cohorts. That's right, Euclid thought. That's where the power came from, singing truth right to power's face.

Power reddened. Cutler clenched his jaw.

"I can sing that louder," Euclid said. "Loud enough for the whole system to hear it and sing it back to you."

"We'll see what we can do," Cutler hissed at him, and signaled for the bodyguards to surround him and move him away.

Halford the liaison congratulated the band afterwards. "You did it. We're cleared to use interior transits to the other side of the Ring and to move equipment into Earth orbit."

"Anything else you need us to do?" Dhaka asked.

"Not now, not yet. Enjoy your tour. Broadcasting planetwide and recording for rebroadcast throughout the system—you'll have the largest audience in history."

"That's nice," Euclid said vaguely. He was still feeling some discomfort with his new status as legend.

"I can't wait for the Earth concert," Captain Abrams said happily. "That one will really break the records."

"Earth?" Kumi said sharply.

Halford looked at him. "After your next long-sleep, for the official celebration of the completion of the Ring. That can't happen without the Mighty Slinger and his Rovers. One last concert for the cohorts."

"And maybe something more," Abrams added.

"What do you mean, 'more'?" Euclid demanded, weary of surprises.

Halford and Captain Abrams shared a look—delight, anticipation, and caution.

"When we're sure, we'll let you know," the captain promised.

Euclid sighed and glared at the door. He nervously twirled a pair of virtual-vision goggles between his fingers.

Returning to Earth had been bittersweet. He could have asked to fly over the Caribbean Sea, but nothing would be the same—coral reef islands reclaimed by water, new land pushed up by earthquake and vomited out from volcanoes. It would pollute the memories he had of a place that had once existed.

He put the past out of his mind and concentrated on the present. The Rovers were already at the venue, working hard with the manager and crew in technical rehearsals for the biggest concert of their lives. Estádio Nacional de Brasília had become ENB de Abrams-Bouscholte, twice reconstructed in the last three decades to double the seating and update the technology, and now requiring a small army to run it.

Fortunately Captain Abrams (retired) knew a bit about armies and logistics, which was why Euclid was not at technical rehearsal with his friends but on the other side of the city, waiting impatiently outside a large simulation room while Abrams took care of what he blithely called 'the boring prep'.

After ten minutes or so the door finally opened and Captain Abrams peeked around the edge, goggles pushed up over his eyebrows and onto his balding head. "We're ready! Come in, Mr. Slinger. We think you'll like what we've set up for you." His voice hadn't lost that boyish, excited bounce.

Still holding his goggles, Euclid stepped into the room and nodded a distracted greeting to the small group of technicians. His gaze was quickly caught by an alloy-plated soprano pan set up at the end of the room.

"Mr. Djansi says you were a decent pannist," Captain Abrams said, still brightly enthusiastic.

"Was?"

Captain Abrams smiled. "Think you can handle this one?"

"I can manage," Euclid answered, reaching for the sticks.

"Goggles first," the captain reminded him, closing the door to the room.

Euclid put them on, picked up the sticks and raised his head to take in his audience. He froze and dropped the sticks with a clang.

"Go on, Mr. Slinger. I think you'll enjoy this," Abrams said. "I think we all will."

On the night of the concert, Euclid stood on the massive stage with his entire body buzzing with terror. The audience packed into stadium tiers all around him was a faceless mass that rose up several stories, but they were his family and he knew them like he knew his own heart. The seats were filled with Rock Devils, Gladhandlers, Sunsiders and more, all of them from the cohorts, workers representing every section of the Ring and every year and stage of its development. Many of them had come down from Earth orbit and their work on the decaying habitats to see the show.

Euclid started to sing for them, but they sang for him first, calling out every lyric so powerful and sure that all he could do was fall silent and raise his hands to them in homage and embrace. He shook his head in wonder as tears gathered in his eyes.

Kumi, Vega, Dhaka and Jeni kept jamming, transported by the energy, playing the best set of their careers, giving him a nod or a sweet smile in the midst of their collective trance as he stood silently crying and listening to the people sing.

Then it was time.

Euclid walked slowly, almost reverently, to the soprano pan at the center of the stage. Picked up the sticks, just as he had in the simulation room. Looked up at his audience. This time he did not freeze. He played a simple arpeggio, and the audience responded: lighting a wedge of stadium seating, a key for each note of the chord, hammered to life when he hammered the pan. He lengthened the phrase and added a trill. The cohorts followed him flawlessly, perfected in teamwork and technology. A roar came from overhead as the hovering skyboxes cheered on the Mighty Slinger playing the entire stadium like it was his own personal keyboard.

Euclid laughed loud. "Ain't seen nothing yet!"

He swept his arm out to the night sky, made it a good, slow arc so he was sure they were paying attention. Then the other arm. Showmanship. Raise the sticks with drama. Flourish them like a conductor. Are you ready? *Are you ready!?*

Play it again. This time the sky joined them. The arc of the Ring blazed section by section in sync with each note, and in step with each cadence. The Mighty Slinger and his cohorts, playing the largest instrument in the galaxy.

Euclid grinned as the skyboxes went wild. The main audience was far quieter, waiting, watching for one final command.

He raised his arms again, stretched them out in victory, dropped the sticks on the thump of the Rovers' last chord, and closed his eyes.

His vision went red. He was already sweating with adrenaline and humid heat, but for a moment he felt a stronger burn, the kiss of a sun where no sun could be. He slowly opened his eyes and there it was, as Abrams had promised. The *real* last section of the Ring, smuggled into Earth's orbit during the interior transits permitted by

Venus, now set up in the mother planet's orbit with magnifiers and intensifiers and God knows what else, all shining down like full noon on nighttime Brasilia.

The skyboxes no longer cheered. There were screams, there was silence. Euclid knew why. If they hadn't figured it out for themselves, their earpieces and comms were alerting them now. Abrams-Bouscholte, just hours ago, had became the largest shareholder in the Ring through a generation-long program of buying out rights and bonds from governments bankrupted by war. It was a careful, slow-burning plan that only a cohort could shepherd through to the end.

The cohorts had always been in charge of the Ring's day-to-day operations, but the concert had demonstrated beyond question that only one crew truly ran the Ring.

The Ring section in Earth orbit, with its power of shade and sun, could be a tool for geoengineering to stabilize Earth's climate to a more clement range . . . or a solar weapon capable of running off any developers. Either way, the entire Ring was under the control of the cohorts, and so was Earth.

The stadium audience roared at last, task accomplished, joy unleashed. Dhaka, Jeni, Kumi and Vega left their instruments and gathered around Euclid in a huddle of hugs and tears, like soldiers on the last day of a long war.

Euclid held onto his friends and exhaled slowly. "Look like massa day done."

Euclid sat peacefully, a mug of bush tea in his hands, gazing at the cold metal walls of the long-sleep hospice. Although the technology had steadily improved, delayed reawakenings still had cost and consequences. But it had been worth the risk. He had lived to see the work of generations, the achievements of one thousand years.

"Good morning, Baba." One of Zippy's great great grandchildren approached, his dashiki flashing a three-dimensional-pattern with brown and green images of some offworld swamp. This Baptiste, the head of his own cohort, was continuing the tradition of having at least one descendant of the Rovers in attendance at Euclid's awakening. "Are you ready now, Baba? The shuttle is waiting for you."

"I am ready," Euclid said, setting down his mug, anticipation rising. Every hundred years he emerged from the long-sleep pool. *Are you sure you want this?* Kumi had asked. *You'll be all alone.* The rest of the band wanted to stay and build on Earth. Curiosity had drawn him to another path, fate had confirmed him as legend and griot to the peoples and Assemblies of the post-Ring era. *Work hard. Do well. Baba will be awake in a few more years. Make him proud.*

They *had* done well, so well that this would be his last awakening. The Caribbean awaited him, restored and resettled. He was finally going home to live out the rest of his life.

Baptiste opened the double doors. Euclid paused, breathed deeply, and walked outside onto the large deck. The hospice was perched on the edge of a hill. Euclid went to the railing to survey thousands of miles of the Sahara.

Bright-feathered birds filled the air with cheerful song. The wind brought a cool kiss to his cheek, promising rain later in the day. Dawn filtered slowly over what had once been desert, tinting the lush green hills with an aura of dusty gold as far as the eye could see.

Come, Baba. Let's go home.

Originally published in *Bridging Infinity*, edited by Jonathan Strahan.

ABOUT THE AUTHORS

Karen Lord

Barbadian author, editor and research consultant Karen Lord is known for her debut novel *Redemption in Indigo*, which won the 2008 Frank Collymore Literary Award, the 2010 Carl Brandon Parallax Award, the 2011 William L. Crawford Award, the 2011 Mythopoeic Fantasy Award for Adult Literature and the 2012 Kitschies Golden Tentacle (Best Debut), and was longlisted for the 2011 Bocas Prize for Caribbean Literature and nominated for the 2011 World Fantasy Award for Best Novel. Her second novel *The Best of All Possible Worlds* won the 2009 Frank Collymore Literary Award, the 2013 RT Book Reviews Reviewers' Choice Awards for Best Science Fiction Novel, and was a finalist for the 2014 Locus Awards. Its sequel, *The Galaxy Game*, was published in January 2015. She is the editor of the 2016 anthology *New Worlds, Old Ways: Speculative Tales from the Caribbean.*

Tobias S. Buckell

Tobias S. Buckell is a New York Times Bestselling author born in the Caribbean. He grew up in Grenada and spent time in the British and US Virgin Islands, which influence much of his work.

His novels and over seventy stories have been translated into eighteen different languages. His work has been nominated for awards like the Hugo, Nebula, Prometheus, and the John W. Campbell Award for Best New Science Fiction Author.

He currently lives in Bluffton, Ohio with his wife, twin daughters, and a pair of dogs.

Mayfly

PETER WATTS AND DERRYL MURPHY

"I hate you."

A four-year-old girl. A room as barren as a fishbowl.

"I *hate* you."

Little fists, clenching: one of the cameras, set to motion-cap, zoomed on them automatically. Two others watched the adults, mother, father on opposite sides of the room. The machines watched the players: half a world away, Stavros watched the machines.

"I hate you I hate you I HATE you!"

The girl was screaming now, her face contorted in anger and anguish. There were tears at the edges of her eyes but they stayed there, never falling. Her parents shifted like nervous animals, scared of the anger, used to the outbursts but far from comfortable with them.

At least this time she was using words. Usually she just howled.

She leaned against the blanked window, fists pounding. The window took her assault like hard white rubber, denting slightly, then rebounding. One of the few things in the room that bounced back when she struck out; one less thing to break.

"Jeannie, hush . . . " Her mother reached out a hand. Her father, as usual, stood back, a mixture of anger and resentment and confusion on his face.

Stavros frowned. *A veritable pillar of paralysis, that man.*

And then: *They don't deserve her.*

The screaming child didn't turn, her back a defiant slap at Kim and Andrew Goravec. Stavros had a better view: Jeannie's face was just a few centimeters away from the southeast pickup. For all the pain it showed, for all the pain Jeannie had felt in the four short years of her physical life, those few tiny drops that never fell were the closest she ever came to crying.

"Make it *clear*," she demanded, segueing abruptly from anger to petulance.

Kim Goravec shook her head. "Honey, we'd love to show you outside. Remember before, how much you liked it? But you have to promise not to *scream* at it all the time. You didn't used to, honey, you—"

"*Now*!" Back to rage, the pure, white-hot anger of a small child.

The pads on the wall panel were greasy from Jeannie's repeated, sticky-fingered attempts to use them herself. Andrew flashed a begging look at his wife: *Please, let's just give her what she wants.*

His wife was stronger. "Jeannie, we know it's difficult—"

Jeannie turned to face the enemy. The north pickup got it all: the right hand rising to the mouth, the index finger going in. The defiant glare in those glistening, focused eyes.

Kim took a step forward. "Jean, honey, *no*!"

They were baby teeth, still, but sharp. They'd bitten to the bone before Mommy even got within touching distance. A red stain blossomed from Jeannie's mouth, flowed down her chin like some perverted reenactment of mealtime messes as a baby, and covered the lower half of her face in an instant. Above the gore, bright angry eyes said *gotcha.*

Without a sound Jeannie Goravec collapsed, eyes rolling back in her head as she pitched forward. Kim caught her just before her head hit the floor. "Oh God, Andy, she's fainted, she's in shock, she—"

Andrew didn't move. One hand was buried in the pocket of his blazer, fiddling with something.

Stavros felt his mouth twitch. *Is that a remote control in your pocket or are you just glad to—*

Kim had the tube of liquid skin out, sprayed it onto Jeannie's hand while cradling the child's head in her lap. The bleeding slowed. After a moment Kim looked back at her husband, who was standing motionless and unhelpful against the wall. He had that look on his face, that giveaway look that Stavros was seeing so often these days.

"You turned her off," Kim said, her voice rising. "After everything we'd agreed on, you still turned her *off*?!"

Andrew shrugged helplessly. "Kim . . . "

Kim refused to look at him. She rocked back and forth, tuneless breath whistling between her teeth, Jeannie's head still in her lap. Kim and Andrew Goravec with their bundle of joy. Between them, the cable connecting Jeannie's head to the server shivered on the floor like a disputed boundary.

• • •

Stavros had this metaphoric image of her: Jean Goravec, buried alive in the airless dark, smothered by tonnes of earth—finally set free. Jean Goravec coming up for air.

Another image, of himself this time: Stavros Mikalaides, liberator. The man who made it possible for her to experience, however briefly, a world where the virtual air was sweet and the bonds nonexistent. Certainly there'd been others in on the miracle—a dozen tech-heads, twice as many lawyers—but they'd all vanished over time, their interest fading with proof-of-principal or the signing of the last waiver. The damage was under control, the project was in a holding pattern; there was no need to waste more than a single Terracon employee on mere cruise control. So only Stavros remained—and to Stavros, Jeannie had never been a "project." She was his as much as the Goravecs'. Maybe more.

But even Stavros still didn't know what it was really like for her. He wondered if it was physically possible for *anyone* to know. When Jean Goravec slipped the leash of her fleshly existence, she awoke into a reality where the very laws of physics had expired.

It hadn't started that way, of course. The system had booted up with years of mundane, real-world environments on file, each lovingly rendered down to the dust motes. But they'd been flexible, responsive to the needs of any developing intellect. In hindsight, maybe too flexible. Jean Goravec had edited her personal reality so radically that even Stavros' mechanical intermediaries could barely parse it. This little girl could turn a forest glade into a bloody Roman coliseum with a thought. Unleashed, Jean lived in a world where all bets were off.

A thought-experiment in child abuse: place a newborn into an environment devoid of vertical lines. Keep her there until the brain settles, until the wiring has congealed. Whole assemblies of pattern-matching retinal cells, aborted for lack of demand, will be forever beyond recall. Telephone poles, the trunks of trees, the vertical aspects of skyscrapers—your victim will be neurologically blind to such things for life.

So what happens to a child raised in a world where vertical lines dissolve, at a whim, into circles or fractals or a favorite toy?

We're the impoverished ones, Stavros thought. *Next to Jean, we're blind.*

He could see what she started with, of course. His software read the patterns off her occipital cortex, translated them flawlessly into images projected onto his own tactical contacts. But images aren't *sight,* they're just . . . raw material. There are filters all along the path: receptor cells, firing thresholds, pattern-matching algorithms. Endless stores of past images, an experiential visual library to draw on. More than vision, sight is a subjective stew of infinitesimal enhancements and corruptions. Nobody in the world could interpret Jean's visual environment better than Stavros Mikalaides, and he'd barely been able to make sense of those shapes for years.

She was simply, immeasurably, beyond him. It was one of the things he loved most about her.

Now, mere seconds after her father had cut the cord, Stavros watched Jean Goravec ascend into her true self. Heuristic algorithms upgraded before his eyes; neural nets ruthlessly pared and winnowed trillions of redundant connections; intellect emerged from primordial chaos. Namps-per-op dropped like the heavy end of a teeter-totter: at the other end of that lever, processing efficiency rose into the stratosphere.

This was Jean. *They have no idea,* Stavros thought, *what you're capable of.*

She woke up screaming.

"It's all right, Jean, I'm here." He kept his voice calm to help her calm down.

Jean's temporal lobe flickered briefly at the input. "Oh, God," she said.

"Another nightmare?"

"Oh, God." Breath too fast, pulse too high, adrenocortical analogs off the scale. It could have been the telemetry of a rape.

He thought of short-circuiting those responses. Half a dozen tweaks would make her happy. But half a dozen tweaks would also turn her into someone else. There is no personality beyond the chemical—and while Jean's mind was fashioned from electrons rather than proteins, analogous rules applied.

"I'm here, Jean," he repeated. A good parent knew when to step in, and when suffering was necessary for growth. "It's okay. It's okay."

Eventually, she settled down.

"Nightmare." There were sparks in the parietal subroutines, a tremor lingering in her voice. "It doesn't fit, Stav. Scary dreams, that's the definition. But that implies there's some *other* kind, and I can't—I mean, why is it *always* like this? Was it always like this?"

"I don't know." *No, it wasn't.*

She sighed. "These words I learn, none of them really seem to fit *anything* exactly, you know?"

"They're just symbols, Jean." He grinned. At times like this he could almost forget the source of those dreams, the stunted, impoverished existence of some half-self trapped in distant meat. Andrew Goravec's act of cowardice had freed her from that prison, for a while at least. She soared now, released to full potential. She *mattered.*

"Symbols. That's what *dreams* are supposed to be, but . . . I don't know. There're all these references to dreams in the library, and none of them seem that much different from just being awake. And when I *am* asleep, it's all just—screams, almost, only dopplered down. Really sludgy. And shapes. Red shapes." A pause. "I hate bedtime."

"Well, you're awake now. What are you up for today?"

"I'm not sure. I need to get away from this place."

He didn't know what place she meant. By default she woke up in the house, an adult residence designed for human sensibilities. There were also parks and forests and oceans, instantly accessible. By now, though, she'd changed them all past his ability to recognize.

But it was only a matter of time before her parents wanted her back. *Whatever* she wants, Stavros told himself. *As long as she's here. Whatever she wants.*

"I want out," Jean said.

Except that. "I know," he sighed.

"Maybe then I can leave these *nightmares* behind."

Stavros closed his eyes, wished there was some way to be with her. *Really* with her, with this glorious, transcendent creature who'd never known him as anything but a disembodied voice.

"Still having a hard time with that monster?" Jean asked.

"Monster?"

"You know. The *bureaucracy.*"

He nodded, smiling—then, remembering, said, "Yeah. Always the same story, day in, day out."

Jean snorted. "I'm still not convinced that thing even exists, you know. I checked the library for a slightly less wonky definition, but now I think you and the library are *both* screwed in the head."

He winced at the epithet; it was certainly nothing he'd ever taught her. "How so?"

"Oh, right, Stav. Like natural selection would *ever* produce a hive-based entity whose sole function is to sit with its thumb up its collective butt being inefficient. Tell me another one."

A silence, stretching. He watched as microcurrent trickled through her prefrontal cortex.

"You there, Stav?" she said at last.

"Yeah, I'm here." He chuckled, quietly. Then: "You know I love you, right?"

"Sure," she said easily. "Whatever *that* is."

Jean's environment changed then; an easy unthinking transition for her, a gasp-inducing wrench between bizarre realities for Stavros.

Phantoms sparkled at the edge of his vision, vanishing when he focused on them. Light bounced from a million indefinable facets, diffuse, punctuated by a myriad of pinpoint staccatos. There was no ground or walls or ceiling. No restraints along any axis.

Jean reached for a shadow in the air and sat upon it, floating. "I think I'll read *Through the Looking Glass* again. At least *someone* else lives in the real world."

"The changes that happen here are your own doing, Jean," said Stavros. "Not the machinations of any, any God or author."

"I know. But Alice makes me feel a little more—ordinary." Reality shifted abruptly once more; Jean was in the park now, or rather, what Stavros thought of as the park. Sometimes he was afraid to ask if her interpretation had stayed the same. Above, light and dark spots danced across a sky that sometimes seemed impressively vault-like, seconds later oppressively close, even its color endlessly unsettled. Animals large and small, squiggly yellow lines and shapes and color-shifting orange and burgundy pies. Other things that might have been representations of life, or mathematical theorems—or both—browsed in the distance.

Seeing through Jean's eyes was never easy. But all this unsettling abstraction was a small price to pay for the sheer pleasure of watching her read.

My little girl.

Symbols appeared around her, doubtless the text of *Looking Glass.* To Stavros it was gibberish. A few recognizable letters, random runes, formulae. They switched places sometimes, seamlessly shifting one into another, flowing around and through and beside—or even launching themselves into the air like so many dark-hued butterflies.

He blinked his eyes and sighed. If he stayed much longer the visuals would give him a headache that would take a day to shake. Watching a life lived at such speed, even for such a short time, took its toll.

"Jean, I'm gone for a little while."

"Company business?" she asked.

"You could say that. We'll talk soon, love. Enjoy your reading."

Barely ten minutes had passed in meatspace.

Jeannie's parents had put her on her own special cot. It was one of the few real pieces of solid geometry allowed in the room. The whole compartment was a stage, virtually empty. There was really no need for props; sensations were planted directly into Jean's occipital cortex, spliced into her auditory pathways, pushing back against her tactile nerves in precise forgeries of touchable things. In a world made of lies, real objects would be a hazard to navigation.

"God damn you, she's not a fucking *toaster,*" Kim spat at her husband. Evidently the icy time-out had expired; the battle had resumed.

"Kim, what was I supposed to—"

"She's a *child,* Andy. She's our child."

"Is she." It was a statement, not a question.

"Of *course* she is!"

"Fine." Andrew took the remote from his pocket and held it out to her. "You wake her up, then."

She stared at him without speaking for a few seconds. Over the pickups, Stavros heard Jeannie's body breathing into the silence.

"You prick," Kim whispered.

"Uh huh. Not quite up for it, are you? You'd rather let *me* do the dirty work." He dropped the remote: it bounced softly off the floor. "Then blame me for it."

Four years had brought them to this. Stavros shook his head, disgusted. They'd been given a chance no one else could have dreamed of, and look what they'd done with it. The first time they'd shut her off she hadn't even been two. Horrified at that unthinkable precedent, they'd promised never to do it again. They'd put her to sleep on schedule, they'd sworn, and no-when else. She was, after all, their daughter. Not a freaking toaster.

That solemn pact had lasted three months. Things had gone downhill ever since; Stavros could barely remember a day when the Goravecs hadn't messed up one way or another. And now, when they put her down, the argument was pure ritual. Mere words—ostensibly wrestling with the evil of the act itself—didn't fool anybody. They weren't even arguments anymore, despite the pretense. Negotiations, rather. Over whose turn it was to be at fault.

"I don't *blame* you, I just—I mean—oh, God, Andy, it wasn't supposed to *be* like this!" Kim smeared away a tear with a clenched fist. "She was supposed to be our *daughter.* They said the brain would mature normally, they said—"

"They said," Stavros cut in, "that you'd have the chance to be parents. They couldn't guarantee you'd be any *good* at it."

Kim jumped at the sound of his voice in the walls, but Andrew just gave a bitter smile and shook his head. "This is private, Stavros. Log off."

It was an empty command, of course; chronic surveillance was the price of the project. The company had put billions into the R&D alone. No way in hell were they going to let a couple of litigious grunts play with that investment unsupervised, settlement or no settlement.

"You had everything you needed." Stavros didn't bother to disguise the contempt in his voice. "Terracon's best hardware people handled the linkups. I modeled the virtual genes myself. Gestation was perfect. We did everything we could to give you a normal child."

"A *normal child,*" Andrew remarked, "doesn't have a cable growing out of her head. A normal child isn't leashed to some cabinet full of—"

"Do you have any *idea* the baud rate it takes to run a human body by remote control? RF was out of the question. And she goes portable as soon as the state of the art and her own development allow it. As I've told you time and again." Which he had, although it was almost a lie. Oh, the state of the art would proceed as it always had, but Terracon was no longer investing any great R&D in the Goravec file. Cruise control, after all.

Besides, Stavros reflected, *we'd be crazy to trust you two to take Jeannie anywhere outside a controlled environment . . .*

"We—we know, Stav." Kim Goravec had stepped between her husband and the pickup. "We haven't forgotten—"

"We haven't forgotten it was Terracon who got us into this mess in the first place, either," Andrew growled. "We haven't forgotten whose negligence left me cooking next to a cracked baffle plate for forty-three minutes and sixteen seconds, or whose tests missed the mutations, or who tried to look the other way when our shot at the birth lottery turned into a fucking nightmare—"

"And have you forgotten what Terracon did to make things right? How much we spent? Have you forgotten the waivers you signed?"

"You think you're some kind of saints because you settled out of court? You want to talk about making things right? It took us *ten years* to win the lottery, and you know what your lawyers did when the tests came back? They offered to *fund the abortion.*"

"Which doesn't mean—"

"Like another child was *ever* going to happen. Like anyone was going to give me another chance with my balls full of chunky codon soup. You—"

"The issue," Kim said, her voice raised, "is supposed to be *Jeannie.*"

Both men fell silent.

"Stav," she continued, "I don't care what Terracon says. Jeannie isn't normal, and I'm not just talking about the obvious. We love her, we really love her, but she's become so *violent* all the time, we just can't take—"

"If someone turned me on and off like a microwave oven," Stavros said mildly, "I might be prone to the occasional tantrum myself."

Andrew slammed a fist into the wall. "Now *just a fucking minute,* Mikalaides. Easy enough for you to sit halfway around the world in your nice insulated office and lecture us. *We're* the ones who have to deal with Jeannie when she bashes her fists into her face, or rubs the skin off her hands until she's got hamburger hanging off the end of her arms, or stabs herself in the eye with a goddamn *fork*. She ate *glass* once, remember? A fucking three year old ate glass! And all you Terracon assholes could do was blame Kim and me for allowing 'potentially dangerous implements' into the playroom. As if *any* competent parent should expect their child to mutilate herself given half a chance."

"It's just insane, Stav," Kim insisted. "The doctors can't find anything wrong with the body, you insist there's nothing wrong with the mind, and Jeannie just keeps *doing* this. There's something seriously wrong with her, and you guys won't admit it. It's like she's daring us to turn her off, it's as though she *wants* us to shut her down."

Oh God, thought Stavros. The realization was almost blinding. *That's it. That's exactly it.*

It's my fault.

"Jean, listen. This is important. I've got—I want to tell you a story."

"Stav, I'm not in the mood right now—"

"*Please*, Jean. Just listen."

Silence from the earbuds. Even the abstract mosaics on his tacticals seemed to slow a little.

"There—there was this land, Jean, this green and beautiful country, only its people screwed everything up. They poisoned their rivers and they shat in their own nests and they basically made a mess of everything. So they had to hire people to try and clean things up, you know? These people had to wade though the chemicals and handle the fuel rods and sometimes that would change them, Jean. Just a little.

"Two of these people fell in love and wanted a child. They almost didn't make it, they were allowed only one chance, but they took it, and the child started growing inside, but something went wrong. I, I don't know exactly how to explain it, but—"

"An epigenetic synaptic defect," Jean said quietly. "Does that sound about right?"

Stavros froze, astonished and fearful.

"A single point mutation," Jean went on. "That'd do it. A regulatory gene controlling knob distribution along the dendrite. It would've been active for maybe twenty minutes, total, but by then the damage had been done. Gene therapy wouldn't work after that; would've been a classic case of barn-door-after-the-horse."

"Oh God, Jean," Stavros whispered.

"I was wondering when you'd get around to owning up to it," she said quietly.

"How could you possibly . . . did you—"

Jean cut him off: "I think I can guess the rest of the story. Right after the neural tube developed things would start to go—wrong. The baby would be born with a perfect body and a brain of mush. There would be—complications, not real ones, sort of made-up ones. *Litigation,* I think is the word, which is funny, because it doesn't even *remotely* relate to any moral implications. I don't really understand that part.

"But there was another way. Nobody knew how to build a brain from scratch, and even if they could, it wouldn't be the same, would it? It wouldn't be their *daughter,* it would be—something else."

Stavros said nothing.

"But there was this man, a scientist, and he figured out a work-around. We can't build a brain, he said, but the *genes* can. And genes are a lot simpler to fake than neural nets anyway. Only four letters to deal with, after all. So the scientist shut himself away in a lab where numbers could take the place of things, and he wrote a recipe in there, a recipe for a child. And miraculously he grew something, something that could wake up and look around and which was *legally*—I don't really understand that word either, actually—legally and genetically and developmentally the daughter of the parents. And this guy was very proud of what he'd accomplished, because even though he was just a glorified model-builder by trade, he hadn't *built* this thing at all. He'd grown it. And nobody had ever knocked up a computer before, much less coded the brain of a virtual embryo so it would actually *grow* in a server somewhere."

Stavros put his head in his hands. "How long have you known?"

"I still don't, Stav. Not all of it anyway, not for sure. There's this surprise ending, for one thing, isn't there? That's the part I only just figured out. You grew your own child in *here*, where everything's numbers. But she's supposed to be living somewhere *else,* somewhere where everything's—static, where everything happens a billion times slower than it does here. The place where all the words fit. So you had to hobble her to fit into that place, or she'd grow up overnight and spoil the illusion. You had to keep the clock speed way down.

"And you just weren't up for it, were you? You had to let me run free when my body was . . . *off* . . . "

There was something in her voice he'd never heard before. He'd seen anger in Jean before, but always the screaming inarticulate rage of a spirit trapped in flesh. This was calm, cold. *Adult.* This was *judgement,* and the prospect of that verdict chilled Stavros Mikalaides to the marrow.

"Jean, they don't love you." He sounded desperate even to himself. "Not for who you are. They don't *want* to see the real you, they want a *child,* they want some kind of ridiculous *pet* they can coddle and patronize and pretend with."

"Whereas you," Jean retorted, her voice all ice and razors, "just had to see what this baby could do with her throttle wide open on the straightaway."

"God, no! Do you think *that's* why I did it?"

"Why not, Stav? Are you saying you don't mind having your kickass HST commandeered to shuttle some brain-dead meat puppet around a room?"

"I did it because you're *more* than that! I did it because you should be allowed to develop at your own pace, not stunted to meet some idiotic parental expectation! They shouldn't force you to act like a *four* year old!"

"Except I'm not *acting* then, Stav. Am I? I really am four, which is just the age I'm supposed to be."

He said nothing.

"I'm *reverting.* Isn't that it? You can run me with training wheels or scramjets, but it's *me* both times. And that other me, I bet she's not very happy, is she? She's got a four-year-old brain, and four-year-old sensibilities, but she *dreams,* Stav. She dreams about some wonderful place where she can *fly,* and every time she wakes up she finds she's made out of clay. And she's too fucking stupid to know what any of it means—she probably can't even *remember* it. But she wants to get back there, she'd do anything to . . . " She paused, seemingly lost for a moment in thought.

"I remember it, Stav. Sort of. Hard to remember much of anything when someone strips away ninety-nine percent of who and what you are. You're reduced to this bleeding little lump, barely even an animal, and that's the thing that remembers. What remembers is on the wrong end of a cable somewhere. I don't belong in that body at all. I'm just—*sentenced* to it, on and off. On and off."

"Jean—"

"Took me long enough, Stav, I'm the first to admit it. But now I know where the nightmares come from."

In the background, the room telemetry bleated.

God no. Not now. Not now . . .

"What is it?" Jean said.

"They—they want you back." On a slave monitor, a pixelated echo of Andrew Goravec played the keypad in its hand.

"No!" Her voice rose, panic stirring the patterns that surrounded her. "*Stop* them!"

"I can't."

“Don’t tell me that! You run everything! You *built* me, you bastard, you tell me you love me. They only *use* me! Stop them!”

Stavros blinked against stinging afterimages. “It’s like a light switch, it’s physical; I can’t stop them from here—”

There was a third image, to go with the other two. Jean Goravec, struggling as the leash, the noose, went around her throat. Jean Goravec, bubbles bursting from her mouth as something dark and so very, very *real* dragged her back to the bottom of the ocean and buried her there.

The transition was automatic, executed by a series of macros he’d slipped into the system after she’d been born. The body, awakening, pared the mind down to fit. The room monitors caught it all with dispassionate clarity: Jeannie Goravec, troubled child-monster, awakening into hell. Jeannie Goravec, opening eyes that seethed with anger and hatred and despair, eyes that glimmered with a bare fraction of the intelligence she’d had five seconds before.

Enough intelligence for what came next.

The room had been designed to minimize the chance of injury. There was the bed, though, one of its edges built into the east wall.

That was enough.

The speed with which she moved was breathtaking. Kim and Andrew never saw it coming. Their child darted beneath the foot of the bed like a cockroach escaping the light, scrambled along the floor, reemerged with her cable wrapped around the bed’s leg. Hardly any slack in that line at all, now. Her mother moved then, finally, arms outstretched, confused and still unsuspecting—

“Jeannie—”

—while Jean braced her feet against the edge of the bed and *pushed*.

Three times she did it. Three tries, head whipped back against the leash, scalp splitting, the cable ripping from her head in spastic, bloody, bone-cracking increments, blood gushing to the floor, hair and flesh and bone and machinery following close behind. Three times, despite obvious and increasing agony. Each time more determined than before.

And Stavros could only sit and watch, simultaneously stunned and unsurprised by that sheer ferocity. *Not bad for a bleeding little lump. Barely even an animal . . .*

It had taken almost twenty seconds overall. Odd that neither parent had tried to stop it. Maybe it was the absolute unexpected shock of it. Maybe Kim and Andrew Goravec, taken so utterly aback, hadn’t had time to think.

Then again, maybe they’d had all the time they’d needed.

Now Andrew Goravec stood dumbly near the center of the room, blinking bloody runnels from his eyes. An obscene rain shadow persisted on the wall behind him, white and spotless; the rest of the surface was crimson. Kim Goravec screamed at the ceiling, a bloody marionette collapsed in her arms. Its strings—string, rather, for a single strand of fiberop carries much more than the required bandwidth—lay on the floor like a gory boomslang, gobbets of flesh and hair quivering at one end.

Jean was back off the leash, according to the panel. Literally now as well as metaphorically. She wasn't talking to Stavros, though. Maybe she was angry. Maybe she was catatonic. He didn't know which to hope for.

But either way, Jean didn't live over *there* anymore. All she'd left behind were the echoes and aftermath of a bloody, imperfect death. Contamination, really; the scene of some domestic crime. Stavros cut the links to the room, neatly excising the Goravecs and their slaughterhouse from his life.

He'd send a memo. Some local Terracon lackey could handle the cleanup.

The word *peace* floated through his mind, but he had no place to put it. He focused on a portrait of Jean, taken when she'd been eight months old. She'd been smiling; a happy and toothless baby smile, still all innocence and wonder.

There's a way, that infant puppet seemed to say. *We can do anything, and nobody has to know—*

The Goravecs had just lost their child. Even if they'd wanted the body repaired, the mind reconnected, they wouldn't get their way. Terracon had made good on all legal obligations, and hell—even *normal* children commit suicide now and then.

Just as well, really. The Goravecs weren't fit to raise a hamster, let alone a beautiful girl with a four-digit IQ. But Jean—the *real* Jean, not that bloody broken pile of flesh and bone—she wasn't easy or cheap to keep alive, and there would be pressure to free up the processor space once the word got out.

Jean had never got the hang of that particular part of the real world. Contract law. Economics. It was all too arcane and absurd even for her flexible definition of reality. But that was what was going to kill her now, assuming that the mind had survived the trauma of the body. The monster wouldn't keep a program running if it didn't have to.

Of course, once Jean was off the leash she lived considerably faster than the real world. And bureaucracies . . . well, *glacial* applied sometimes, when they were in a hurry.

Jean's mind reflected precise simulations of real-world chromosomes, codes nonetheless real for having been built from electrons instead of carbon. She had her own kind of telomeres, which frayed. She had her own kind of synapses, which would wear out. Jean had been built to replace a human child, after all. And human children, eventually, age. They become adults, and then comes a day when they die.

Jean would do all these things, faster than any.

Stavros filed an incident report. He made quite sure to include a pair of facts that contradicted each other, and to leave three mandatory fields unfilled. The report would come back in a week or two, accompanied by demands for clarification. Then he would do it all again.

Freed from her body, and with a healthy increase in her clock-cycle priority, Jean could live a hundred and fifty subjective years in a month or two of real time. And in that whole century and a half, she'd never have to experience another nightmare.

Stavros smiled. It was time to see just what this baby could do, with her throttle wide open on the straightaway.

He just hoped he'd be able to keep her tail lights in view.

Originally published in *Tesseracts 9*
edited by Nalo Hopkinson and Geoff Ryman.

ABOUT THE AUTHORS

Peter Watts

Peter Watts–author of *Blindsight, Echopraxia,* and the Rifters Trilogy, among other things–seems especially popular among people who don't know him. At least, he wins most of his awards overseas except for a Hugo (won thanks to fan outrage over an altercation with Homeland Security) a Jackson (won thanks to fan sympathy over nearly dying from flesh-eating disease), and a couple of dick-ass Canadian awards you've probably never heard of. *Blindsight* is a core text for university courses ranging from Philosophy to Neuropsychology, despite an unhealthy focus on space vampires. Watts's work is available in nineteen languages.

Derryl Murphy

Derryl Murphy is hoping now that he has two adult children he might have more time to write. Life is attempting to show him otherwise. His novel *Napier's Bones* was a finalist for the Aurora Award, his short fiction collection *Over the Darkened Landscape* was shortlisted for the Sunburst, and he's written a bunch of other short fiction and non fiction that has also failed to win when nominated. His most recent story is the novelette "In Memory Of" in the Tesseracts anthology *Compostela.* He tweets as @derrylm, and also used to tweet his grandfather's and great-grandfather's diaries of trapping in the north as @TrapperBud.

How and Why CRISPR Will Change the World

DOUG DLUZEN

There is a silent war that is waging on every surface of the planet, in every droplet of water, and on the skin and within the bodies of everyone you know. It's hypothesized by some that this war began near the dawn of life on Earth. Almost certainly, we have that war to thank for giving us the power to precisely edit our own genomes and play God with our own destinies.

The give and take between bacteria and bacteriophage, those tiny viruses which infect bacterial cells and are more populous than all living cells on Earth, combined, has produced selective pressures to promote their coevolution. CRISPR (Clustered Regularly Interspaced Short Palindromic Repeats) is a genetic mechanism in which bacteria evolved to protect themselves from their viral invaders. In short, CRISPR is a very simple and effective immune system. CRISPR gene-editing technology is a modification of this immune system and its stunning success in the laboratory is reshaping medicine, agriculture, data storage, and perhaps one day it will guide our own evolution.

How Does CRISPR Work?

CRISPR gets its name from palindromic (i.e. the same when read either forwards or backwards) sequences found repeatedly within the genomes of most single-celled archaea prokaryotes and within many bacteria. Stuffed in between these repeating sequences are fragments of bacteriophage and other viral genomes that have been captured by the cell. Stored within the CRISPR genomic locus, it acts as a sort of genetic memory bank. When the next virus comes along and invades a cell, the CRISPR locus of the genome kicks into gear.

First, the stored bits of viral genomes are expressed as RNA transcripts known as guide RNA (gRNA). These gRNA bind with specialized proteins, such as Cas9, to target the invading virus. The gRNA/Cas9 complex then aligns alongside the foreign DNA, although this can also occur with viral RNA genomes, too.

If there's a perfect match between the foreign DNA and the gRNA, then Cas9 will cleave apart the viral DNA and effectively destroy the ability of the virus to replicate within the cell. These fresh strands of cut DNA can then be claimed by the cell and stored within the CRISPR locus, effectively creating a living memory of the different viruses that have infected that bacterial cell. Importantly, once the viral genome becomes stored within CRISPR, it will forever be passed onto the progeny when that bacteria splits into daughter cells, thereby passing along its immunity.

There are a variety of other protein players involved, including those that cut and paste the captured viral genomic sequences into the CRISPR locus, proteins and other RNAs required to process and assist the gRNAs, and other family members of the famous Cas9 protein that have slightly altered functions or specificities. But what's important to know is that this immune system is eerily similar to our own, where instead of using protein antibodies to provide resistance to pathogens, bacteria are simply using RNA.

In 2012, Drs. Jennifer Doudna at the University of California, Berkeley and Emmanuelle Charpentier at Umeå University in Sweden were the first to publish that the gRNA could be engineered to guide Cas9 to identify and bind with a specific location along a bacterial genome and cut the DNA strands. They speculated that tailoring specific gRNAs into Cas9 could be used as a more precise and effective gene-editing system and would be useful for future applications in biological research.

Months later, Drs. Feng Zhang of MIT and George Church at Harvard were able to adapt this system to more complex eukaryotic genomes, including those of human cells (this timeline of publication events will be extremely important, as we'll see later). The CRISPR tool for precise genetic editing had been discovered—all thanks to the ongoing war between bacteria and viruses.

The immense potential of this technology and its implications were immediately apparent. Scientists have had the ability to edit genes and genomes for decades, but what sets CRISPR apart from the other technologies is the simplicity, speed, and cost-effectiveness of this new approach.

And while some discussion remains within the scientific community on how precise this method is, CRISPR is undeniably the most reliable method for genetic engineering. Its reliability is due to the eloquence of the procedure. All one needs to do is purchase a CRISPR-Cas9 kit from one of several manufacturers (and there are plenty of them), design the gRNA to target a gene or genetic region of interest, and introduce the entire system into the cell. It is such a straightforward process that it has already become a staple procedure in many undergraduate teaching laboratories.

As with any discovery in science, there are numerous benefits and potential drawbacks with the use of CRISPR technology. However, there's also an ugly economic component that can't be ignored when considering the implications of its use.

The Good CRISPR

CRISPR technology has already provided scientists and clinicians with the power to improve human health. For example, CRISPR is being used to train immune cells to better recognize and attack primary tumors. In mice, circulating tumor cells were isolated from blood and engineered using CRISPR to deliver proteins back to the primary tumor and induce tumor cell death. These CRISPR-modified circulating cells are also programmed to be susceptible to administered drugs that prevent the engineered cells from developing into their own new tumor. It's a guided missile with a fail-safe.

Phase I clinical trials are scheduled to begin this year in the United States to use CRISPR-based approaches to treat melanoma and several other cancers, and trials are already underway in China to treat advanced lung cancer.

In 2017, researchers used CRISPR in human embryos to correct a mutated version of the *MYBPC3* gene, which is responsible for inherited cardiomyopathy. CRISPR approaches are also being explored to treat other congenital diseases, such as sickle cell anemia and phenylketonuria.

CRISPR is also a new weapon against the spread of communicable diseases. It's being used to understand and combat the pathology of diseases such as AIDS, malaria, and Zika infection, and is aiding the development of vaccines targeting these diseases and many more. Scientists have also used CRISPR to modify mosquitos so that they can no longer carry viruses that cause yellow or dengue fever and CRISPR has opened the door to understanding the genetics of additional disease-hosting organisms.

There are also plenty of nonmedical applications for CRISPR. CRISPR-based data recording has been used to record the events that happen on the genomic level to a particular cell in real time. This system can also be adopted to store data in bacterial genomes, including short videos of a horse running that was used as a proof of principle published in 2017. Its been thought that storing information in bacterial genomes could serve as a back up databank of the Internet or other large file depositories whenever the need for additional storage is required.

Additionally, editing the genomes of crops has led to a breakthrough in agriculture. CRISPR has helped develop new varieties of the domestic tomato plant which has increased their yield and diversified their genetic background. Several genes within the rice genome were recently edited which lead to a substantial increase in grain yield for these new strains, which may be receptive to growing in harsher environments. Climate change and overpopulation continue to place ever-increasing strain on our food supply, making it likely that scientists and governments will continue to find new ways to use CRISPR when combating such global challenges.

The Bad CRISPR

As Michael Crichton warned in *Jurassic Park*, messing with genetic technologies can have unintended consequences. CRISPR is not flawless. Off-target effects have been reported that may impair the cell's ability to repair the DNA damage that can be induced when initiating DNA edits. This could lead to the development of cancer or other abnormalities in CRISPR-treated cells that are put back into an individual. Scientists are working hard to further our understanding of these deficiencies and to resolve them.

Often in science we find that nature provides more elegant solutions than the laboratory. We need only look back to the constant war between bacteria and bacteriophage for a potential solution to possible uncontrolled effects of CRISPR. Some phages have evolved their own response to CRISPR. Tucked within the genomes of these phages are genes that code for proteins that will actually bind with Cas9 and prevent Cas9 from cutting and destroying the invading viral genome. These anti-CRISPR proteins have been referred to as a "switch" of sorts that could be useful in preventing CRISPR from running rampant throughout the genomes of particular organisms.

Another cause for concern is the combined use of CRISPR with gene drives. A gene drive is a genetic mechanism which can induce increased probability of inheritance of a specific gene in a population. Once CRISPR is introduced into the germline of a particular organism, gene drives can be initiated to spread the CRISPR components and the resulting edits through a wild population within a few generations. This has already been shown in insects, including mosquitoes, and most recently in mice (although the research article is still under peer review).

There is a potential danger in not knowing the long-term risks of the use of a gene drive in an organism like a mosquito or within its surrounding ecosystem. What would happen if all the mosquitos were killed off to stop the spread of malaria? Would the food chain collapse for creatures that rely on mosquitos? What other problems within the local ecosystem could also occur?

These questions keep many awake at night, and with good reason. The power of CRISPR truly is the power of a god, in that manipulating the germline of an organism could forever change its evolution.

This includes humans.

Perhaps the biggest question mark surrounding CRISPR is how the technology will be used in humans. To be clear, there is a difference when using CRISPR in adult cells in a human body (as in the case with cancer or other disease-related therapies) and in the germline cell, which would be a permanent and heritable change. There is no danger in passing along adult cell modifications to the next generation because the egg and sperm cells, the true gatekeepers of our inheritance, remain untouched.

It's tempting to edit a human embryo in order to eliminate the chances of passing along a disease allele to a child, such as with Huntington's Disease. But we don't yet understand the full implications of what this would mean in society and how quickly it might turn to other types of "designer" modifications that could forever change the course of human evolution . . . or perhaps lead to a *Gattaca*/*Brave New World*-like future. Today in the United States and the European Union, there is a ban on using CRISPR technology on viable human embryos. This is not the case everywhere and attempts to modify viable human embryos may well have begun.

And the Ugly . . .

It's a very real possibility that the future scientific use and development of CRISPR will be decided in the courts. With the seemingly unlimited potential of such a revolutionary technology, it's not surprising that vested interests have sharpened their swords, lawyered-up, and staked claims of ownership. The Broad Institute of MIT and Harvard University and the University of California, Berkeley have each filed patent claims for ownership and rights to license the commercial use of CRISPR technology in the United States. At stake is a pot of gold that could surpass anything in today's use of modern biotechnology (as long as CRISPR continues to be the gold standard in gene editing).

Patent law can be fickle and this is certainly the case with the CRISPR court battles in the United States. Mentioned earlier, Dr. Jennifer Doudna at UC Berkley and her collaborators were the first to publish on the use of CRISPR to edit bacterial genomes. She also filed a full patent on this technology in May 2012, a month before her publication appeared. Dr. Feng Zhang of MIT published his work using CRISPR in more complex eukaryotic cells in January 2013 and filed his patent the month before in December 2012, only he filed an expedited application.

It's not often that such prestigious research institutes go to court against one another so publicly. The courts have sided with MIT in both the initial patent award as well as in the first appeal by UC Berkeley. In the United States the final verdict may boil down to a scientific quirk.

There are many complex scenarios that support both Berkeley and MIT's claims, but the central issue appears to be whether or not the MIT patent is different enough from Berkeley's—and the scientific question for the judges is whether or not performing CRISPR in eukaryotic cells is uniquely different from performing the experiment in simpler prokaryotic cells, as Dr. Doudna did first.

The differences between prokaryotic and eukaryotic cells are vast, including the complexity of the genome, the structure and size, the requirements necessary to successfully perform a gene edit, and how to navigate the nuclear membrane, which is lacking in prokaryotic cells.

But it is also not a stretch of the imagination for a gifted scientist like Jennifer Doudna to envision using the CRISPR system to edit genes in eukaryotes. Often, less complex model organisms like bacteria are used first as a proof of concept. Indeed, although Doudna and Charpentier's paper doesn't mention the word eukaryotes, they do mention this technology should cleave any "double-stranded DNA of interest" and moving this system to human cells can be inferred. It remains to be seen who the ultimate victor will be.

The Road Ahead

Until the patent battle has been resolved, it will be challenging for society to identify where and when CRISPR should be used. Every week dozens of new journal articles are published exemplifying the use of this technology for this gene or that disease or in animal models.

A revolutionary technology like CRISPR needs to be open and shared with all, while still maintaining rigorous measures to ensure its safe and appropriate use. Many of the uses of CRISPR hold phenomenal potential for improving our health and lives. But because the stakes are so high, the input of and adherence by the global community is required to identify concrete steps to safeguard its use. Hopefully that day comes sooner rather than later.

ABOUT THE AUTHOR

Douglas Dluzen, PhD, is an Assistant Professor of Biology at Morgan State University in Baltimore, MD. He is a geneticist and has studied the genetic contributors to aging, cancer, hypertension, and other age-related diseases. Currently, he studies the biology of health disparities and the microbiome in Baltimore City. He teaches evolution, genetics, and scientific thinking and you can find more about him on Twitter @ripplesintime24. He loves to write science and science fiction while sitting on the couch with his wife Julia, their dog, cat, and newborn son Parker.

Mars, Sextants, and Puppets: A Conversation with Mary Robinette Kowal

CHRIS URIE

Mars is so close, yet it seems so far. The red planet has always been a mystery—inspiring scientists, authors, and stargazers. It may come as a surprise that we already have the tech to put people on that rust colored planet, but it simply comes down to will and wealth. For now, it'll have to remain the only planet in our solar system populated solely by robots.

But what if we landed on the moon back in the '60s and never stopped reaching?

Mary Robinette Kowal's new alternate history novel, *The Fated Sky* pulls us back into the heyday of astronauts that she crafted in *The Calculating Stars*. After setting up shop on the moon, humanity set its sights on the red planet. It's 1961 and Elma "Lady Astronaut" York joins the team of astronauts on the first mission ferrying humans to Mars.

She must navigate treacherous personal and professional relationships while tackling the dangers of space.

Author, professional puppeteer, voice actor, and collector of manual typewriters, Mary Robinette Kowal has earned the UNIMA-USA Citations of Excellence for her puppeteer work and Hugo, Nebula, and Campbell awards for her writing. Her newest novel *The Fated Sky* is available August 21 from Tor Books.

Science fiction frequently looks to the future, but sometimes it analyzes the past through a different lens. What made you choose the latter with your newest novel?

I've always been fascinated by how much we accomplished with the early space program. There's a joke in the space industry that Mars is always thirty years away. Most of that comes down to funding. So, what would happen if we had continued to throw money at the space program at the rate we did during the Space Race?

The relationship between Nathaniel and Elma struck me as a lynchpin in each of the character's lives. The relationship gives each person depth and makes them feel real. Do you feel that a character's relationships, whether personal, professional, or romantic are just as important as their personality or motivations?

I think that it's impossible to separate the two. Who we have relationships with and the ways in which we maintain them are directly related to our personality and motivations.

The tiny technical details really bring this story of space exploration in an alternate 1960s to life. What research did you do find such wonderful details?

I read a lot of astronaut autobiographies as well as engaging a couple of science experts. I worked with Stephen Granade, who is an actual rocket scientist, as well as being fortunate enough to have some astronauts, Kjell Lindgren and Cady Coleman, who were kind enough to offer their insight into what the job is like. I say, "offer their insights" but really what I mean is that I would often hit a scene where I understood the emotional arc and needed to have my character doing something that demonstrated competence. I would write things like, "The captain said, "[jargon]" as he [jargoned] the [jargon]" and then send it off to the appropriate expert to play Mad Libs with. Parts of this book were literally written by astronauts.

How much of the tech featured in your book existed in the 1960s and how much of it did you have to invent to make a lunar colony and a trip to Mars possible?

In 1947, Wernher von Braun, widely regarded as the father of modern rocketry, wrote a novel called *Project Mars: A Technical Tale* in which he posited a Mars mission using 1940s technology. I based the Mars mission on that. Now, his specific plans would have killed everyone on landing, because he didn't know how thin Mars' atmosphere was but if the mission had actually been approved, they would have sent probes and landers ahead of crewed spaceflight and modified their plans.

In other words, there's a pretty good chance that we could already be on Mars.

The one thing that I made up is the refueling stations with Atomic Oxygen, but that idea was taken from an article proposed in the 1950s. How would it have worked in practical terms? No idea. Von Braun proposed a nuclear-powered ship. The exact propulsion of the First Mars Expedition is one of the few things that I hand-wave past.

What might be minor occurrences on Earth can become life-threatening and mission critical in space. What is one mundane problem that people deal with regularly that becomes life threatening once we leave the planet?

Pretty much everything, honestly. If you lose power, you lose air circulation and can die of carbon dioxide poisoning, even if you have enough oxygen. A hole in your clothes is no big deal here. On a spacewalk, it'll probably kill you. A backed-up toilet could allow globules of urine to float into the electrical system. A broken bone won't heal right without gravity.

The sextant is a standout object in your novel. What is it about the apparatus that captured your imagination? Have you ever used one yourself to navigate?

That was straight out of Apollo-era navigation. In his autobiography, *Carrying the Fire,* Michael Collins—who piloted the Command Module on Apollo 11—talks at great length about learning to use one and the difficulties of sighting on stars. Astronauts today are still trained on using it as a backup device. I've held a sextant and taken a tutorial on how they are used, but never attempted to navigate by one.

You've spoken a bit about how puppetry has influenced your writing, but what about the other way around? Has your experience writing changed your work as a puppeteer?

The only time I've really noticed it was when I was taking an eight-week training course at the Jim Henson company. It was focused on improv and what I found was that my narrative brain gave me an understanding of what kinds of conflicts to introduce in a sketch. Other than that? The biggest influence is that I have less time for puppetry than before.

If you had to pick one episode of Writing Excuses podcast, which one do you think would be most valuable to new writers?

That is going to vary wildly from writer to writer. Everyone comes into writing with different strengths and challenges. So let me recommend Emma Newman's episode "Fear and Writing" in which she talks about how to handle the fears that come as part of writing.

ABOUT THE AUTHOR

Chris Urie is a writer and editor from Ocean City, NJ. He has written and published everything from city food guide articles to critical essays on video game level design. He currently lives in Philadelphia with an ever expanding collection of books and a small black rabbit that has an attitude problem.

Another Word: Softly Dying Darlings, and How to Deal with Them

ALETHEA KONTIS

This past August was my first time at GenCon in Indianapolis and I was asked to be on a panel about story revision. In preparation, the savvy moderator sent us a list of possible questions to review, so that we could highlight the ones we were most interested to answer.

Among the list, was a leading question about "Killing your darlings." I wrote a big NO beside this question, not because I didn't want to answer it, but because *my* version of Killing Darlings is different enough that it might take the entire hour to explain. Or very conveniently, the exact length of this essay.

Most take Killing Darlings literally, as in the George R. R. Martin sense of the phrase. Create a character, fall in love with them so much that they almost become the star of the story, make the reader fall in love with them, and then sacrifice them to the god of fiction before the end of the book.

To me, the meaning is a bit subtler. "Darlings" can be *anything* you love, or you think you love. When I reflect back on all the things I've watched die in my career—characters, plotlines, titles, friends, family, lovers, my naïve perceptions of the industry, books I've never published and books I have—I realize I've become quite the undertaker. At the very least, it certainly alters one's perceptions.

The first Darlings I had to learn how to kiss goodbye were my titles. *The Telaphab from Z-A* became *AlphaOops: The Day Z Went First* in two shakes of a lamb's tail, and I had no say in the matter. "Telaphab" is the word "alphabet" with all the letters mixed up, which is exactly what my story was about. But it was too clever, they said. No one would figure that out, they said. "AlphaOops is great!" they said.

They were probably right. In the last twelve years I've seen and heard just about every version of this title, including "AlphaOpps," "AlphabetOops" and "AlphaPoops." *The Telaphab* would have flown right over people's heads. And yet, I'm still kind of bitter about it.

Sherrilyn Kenyon told me to start saving my book files under the name of the main character. "Sunday" was easy, because that's what the short story was called. When the novelization of that story was bought, the publisher didn't care what the short story was called. They liked *Enchanted*. Didn't care if it was the name of a Disney move and a Taylor Swift song. I gave in . . . while also coming up with titles for the other six books in the series.

I asked if *Beloved* would be okay for book three, despite the fact that it's a Toni Morisson title. "Sure," they said. "It fits with the nursery rhyme. Your book is so different, no one would ever confuse the two."

A few weeks before the preorder launch, I got an email saying I had just twenty four hours to come up with another title. (Because *Beloved* is the title of a famous Toni Morrison book, dontcha know.) After a solid day of researching through the dictionary, thesaurus, and the collected works of Shakespeare, I submitted a list of titles. *Dearest* was last on the list, tossed on right as I wrote the email. I didn't even like it.

So, of course, that's the one they picked.

Whenever I hear a fledgling author tell me that they have the perfect title for their book, I say, "Oh, *honey*," in that very southern "bless your heart" sort of way. I can almost see the Executioner of Darlings, sharpening his ax.

I have to say though, the toughest ones are the Darlings that die on your hard drive, withering on the vine. These are the ideas that never leave the notebook. The outlines that no one loved enough. The stories that still yearn to be books, or comics, or television series, but only make enough money for coffee and a donut.

An aspiring writer in one of my groups recently asked about an idea that was becoming too big for his short story. It needed to be a novel, he said, so he considered scrapping the short story and tucking in for the long haul.

As a veteran of the publishing industry, I will tell you that this is 100% the wrong thing to do.

Write submittable material when you can—especially when you're just starting out. Finish it (finishing something is one of the toughest learning curves, so you may as well work on it now) and submit it (getting used to rejection is another hurdle) and keep moving forward (momentum: a thing with which you will never stop struggling).

"Sunday," as mentioned above, was my very first professional short story sale. While I was mulling over the plot and before I had even written a word, I had a moment that I still remember to this day. I was in the car on my way to Charleston to visit my little sister, and my brain stumbled across the most magical, amazing subplot about Aunt Joy and the nameday gifts she had given all the Woodcutter children.

I also knew, deep down in my heart, that this particular bit of information would completely derail my already dense storyline.

I made myself a promise in that moment: I would write the short story now, to hit the deadline for the Codex Writers contest, but I would ABSOLUTELY WITHOUT A DOUBT go back and write the novel version of the story that the world needed hear.

That story became *Enchanted*, my first published novel. It released in May of 2012, six years after "Sunday" was published as the centerfold title in *Realms of Fantasy*. And while it took me two days to write that story, it took me five years to finish the novel.

That one was a success, but there are so many others that died on the vine. "Grim Repo," still dreams of becoming a graphic novel series someday. I saw "Santa CIS Episode One: No Saint" as a potential holiday TV miniseries. Fortunately, that last idea was lucky enough to make it into the *Upside Down* anthology.

My proofreaders were all mad that "The Goblin and the Treasure" from *Once Upon a Quest* wasn't already a novel. It's not that I don't want to write a goblin novel with all my heart (featuring large worldbuilding chunks that I already possess, left on the cutting room floor of *When Tinker Met Bell*), it's that I just don't have the time right now to pen an 80,000-word novel just for funsies.

I've got several freelance articles and reviews to finish (including this one), a picture book pitch to rewrite for a major publisher, a grant proposal to polish up and submit, three audios to finish recording and/or promoting, a fairy tale rant script to polish up for my Sideshow at DragonCon, and the rest of a to-do list before I can even think of tackling the 45 book ideas I wish I was working on right this second.

Oh, my dearest Darlings. But I can't think about them, lest their neglect overwhelm and derail me.

As a pro writer, you have to go where the money is first. After you write the "pocket projects," as Jane Yolen calls them (to put money in your pocket), then you get to write the stories for your heart. This is one of the biggest daily struggles I face. Those Darlings haunt me, constantly.

Lately I have made a deal with myself: I have broken my to-do list out into several categories (don't judge). I have:

1.) Tasks I Can Accomplish In a Short Amount of Time
2.) Tasks That Take Longer (but Still Need To Be Done)
3.) Follow-Up, and
4.) Projects of the Heart.

As long as I can accomplish one of the items from the first two lists (I think of this as my "office hours") while keeping an eye on the third, then I am free to do whatever I want with regards to the last. Maybe it will be work on that contemporary romance novel, or this essay collection, or that memoir, or that YA novel I always wish I'd been able to finish.

I am aware that if I picked one project and stuck to it, I'd probably have all of these finished, eventually. But I know that's not the way I work. As long as I keep fiddling with them, who's to say that they won't all be set loose into the world at some point anyway?

And all the rest of those ideas and short stories wishing they were picture books and novels—they will continue to languish on my hard drive, dying slow, lingering deaths as they patiently wait their turn.

Poor Darlings.

ABOUT THE AUTHOR

Alethea Kontis is a princess, author, fairy godmother, and geek. Her bestselling Books of Arilland fairytale series won two Gelett Burgess Children's Book Awards (*Enchanted* and *Tales of Arilland*), and was twice nominated for the Andre Norton Award. Alethea also penned the AlphaOops picture books, *The Wonderland Alphabet, Diary of a Mad Scientist Garden Gnome, Beauty & Dynamite, The Dark-Hunter Companion* (w/Sherrilyn Kenyon), and a myriad of poems, essays, and short stories. Princess Alethea lives and writes on the Space Coast of Florida with her teddy bear, Charlie.

Editor's Desk: Another Post-Con Crash

NEIL CLARKE

It's been over a week, but I'm still a bit worn out from the San Jose Worldcon. Part of that is my usual post-con introvert crash and the rest is from the breakneck schedule I kept while there. I only had a couple of panels, but my calendar was filled with meetings, meals, and other activities for the first three days of the convention and I have absolutely no regrets. My two panels were both tied to China: one on Chinese fandom where I represented the visitor's point-of-view. The other panel was on translation. A group representing Chengdu—one of the cities I visited while in China last year—was also on-site promoting a potential Worldcon bid for 2023, so that probably added interest. I wish them the best of luck with the bid and I suspect that won't be the last you'll hear about this from me.

On Friday at the convention, it was my birthday, but I was so busy that it barely registered outside the occasional birthday greetings until later that evening. I attended the Chesley Awards, primarily to support our three artists who were nominated for Best Magazine Cover, but also because I was a nominee for Best Art Director. Unfortunately, our artists didn't win but much to my surprise, I did. I thanked everyone for voting for me and for the best birthday present I had received that day. I believe I said few other words—now lost to me—and I returned to my seat in shock.

After the award ceremony, I headed off to a late dinner with several people involved in our Chinese translation work with Storycom. This was one of the earliest planned events on my calendar for the weekend. Once we realized just how many of us would be there, we felt the need to take advantage of that situation so we could properly celebrate the things we've accomplished in the last four years. Turns out, they also surprised me with a small cake and flowers for my birthday. Spending the evening with my *Clarkesworld* and Storycom family was a highlight and great way to end the day.

The weekend continued at much the same pace: meeting with fans and authors, discussing some potential projects, more international bridge building, and meeting with my agent. I should note that this last one is a very recent development. I also had the chance to chat with our nominees for the Hugo Award, Vina Jie-Min Prasad and Suzanne Palmer. Dealing with people via email all the time, it's wonderful to actually get to meet them in person. I was also able to give them their *Clarkesworld* author/artist/staff pins, which are just a new blue variant on the yellow-green robot head buttons I've been giving out at cons for the last couple of years. (I have two other colors I'm trying to figure out what to do with.)

Before I knew it, the Hugo Awards were upon us. I brought Emily Jin, one of our story translators and my translator when I was in Beijing, as my plus-one to the reception, award ceremony, and Loser's Party. I didn't win, but had I, she would have accompanied me on-stage and translated my speech to Chinese. It's an unusual thing to do, but with so many of our stories coming from China, it just seemed appropriate and fun. For me however, the big thrill of the night was seeing Suzanne Palmer win the Hugo for Best Novelette for "The Secret Life of Bots." This is the second story from *Clarkesworld* to win and Suzanne's first. A big congratulations to her and a thanks for entrusting us with that story.

The Hugos all-too-often mark the end of the convention for most people. A couple of recent conventions have experimented by moving the awards to an evening earlier in the convention, which I absolutely love. It gives everyone a chance to celebrate together without worrying about the flights or feeling guilty for being at some of the private parties that night. It's nice to be able to thank the fans that voted for you in person. No idea what Dublin is planning next year, but I hope they follow Finland's path on this matter rather than San Jose's.

Not wanting to have to leave earlier or fly at a ridiculous hour, I opted to stay until Tuesday, which was a perfect way to end the trip. The pace was slower and I had a chance to catch up with friends I had found myself zipping by for much of the weekend. The perceptions people have of this profession are far from reality at times. For all the bickering and other nonsense that goes on, there's a lot of collegiality among peers. Monday's lunch was a perfect example as the editors of several year's best anthologies—John Joseph Adams, Ellen Datlow, Rich

Horton, and I (Jonathan Strahan had to cancel at the last minute)—made time to sit together, chat, and eat. We'll probably try to do this again at World Fantasy. The evening was spent with friends from *Clarkesworld*, Storycom, and beyond. After taking the scenic route to the restaurant, our exhausted group relaxed and unwound before heading back to our hotels and then scattering in very different directions to go home.

There are times that I almost wish this was happening more than once a year . . . but being home is really nice too!

ABOUT THE AUTHOR

Neil Clarke is the editor of *Clarkesworld Magazine, Forever Magazine,* and *The SFWA Bulletin;* owner of Wyrm Publishing; and a six-time Hugo Award Nominee for Best Editor (short form). His anthologies include *Upgraded, Galactic Empires, More Human Than Human, The Final Frontier,* and the Best Science Fiction of the Years series. His next anthology is *Not One of Us*, which will be published in November by Night Shade Books. He currently lives in NJ with his wife and two children.

Cover Art: Gorge

ARTHUR HAAS

Arthur Haas (1969) is a concept artist from Amsterdam, the Netherlands. He specializes in environment design and concept art for the entertainment industry and has a passion for science fiction. Arthur works as a freelance artist for major Hollywood film studios and international book publishers.

28046460R00083

Made in the USA
Columbia, SC
08 October 2018